Abo

Hello reader! Welcome to the Awakened Series! Whether this is the first book or the last book of this series I feel that it is important to make everyone feel welcome. My name is Wyshana Shivers and I am twenty years old. I was born December 6, 1996 and I have been writing since I was in kindergarten. Writing has always been a passion of mine. I would write stories for hours on end for days at a time. I began this particular series not too long after I graduated high school. There was actually another series that I was in the process of writing, and I ended up losing the notebook with the first book in it. Well, no use crying over spilled milk am I right? So, I began this new series, and fell in love with it. I currently live in South Carolina. I hope you all enjoy reading this story and every other story as much as I enjoyed writing them! The term 'Awakened' is just something that was given to me by Holy Spirit. Yes, I believe in God. Anyway, I guess you can say that this story was God ordained for me to write. I've taken all of the things that I was ever attacked with and combined them into this series. I've taken a very non-traditional approach to the things of God, and as such there are a lot of concepts that may seem unorthodox, or even "Demonic" as some may call it. It's fine if that's your feelings, this series just isn't for you. I encourage you all to seek a relationship with God and find your calling in this life. You only get one, and I suggest you all live it right. But don't get me wrong, you're going to make mistakes and fall short, but that's the good thing about life right? If you still have it, you can fix it. But one thing I will always be sure to have, is faith. Without faith, it is impossible to please God, and without faith, it is impossible for you to achieve your dreams. Do not let anyone tell you what you can and cannot do, if it is your heart's desire, then do it. You don't have to figure it out, God has that covered. And if no one else believes in you, I believe in you. You can accomplish anything! Now without further ado, I give you…. Awakened.

For God, and everyone who supported me.

ISBN 978-1976528484

Chapter 1
"Ignorance is bliss…"

Natori looked out of the window of her class suspiciously. Someone was watching her, but she couldn't see them anywhere. She had been feeling this presence for a while now, prominent enough to notice, but faint enough to remain incognito.

"Damn…" she hissed, brushing her white tresses off of her shoulder.

"Miss Sukimori, is whatever you're observing outside more important than my lesson?" Mr. Stark, her teacher and current bother asked.

Yes. She thought.

"No Mr. Stark." Natori answered, turning her amethyst eyes back to the smart board.

Mr. Stark, a tall, lanky man with thick, chaotic blonde hair and green eyes, turned back to his lecture. The class Natori was currently confined to was Algebra II, the one class she was barely passing. Natori swore Mr. Stark had it out for her, she excelled in all of her other classes, but this was the one class she could study for all night, and still barely make a seventy. She couldn't blame him though, since this was one of the classes she would act out in. But it was only because he droned on and on about nonsense. Liner equations this and logic equations that, perhaps if he made it more interesting than she would be more inclined to learn something.

Natori's tanned skin glowed slightly in the sunlight. A black fishtail vest and black skinny jeans hid her fully developed form from view. Black combat boots completed her outfit and the black snake bites complimented her lips. The more popular girls were skinny, blonde or brunette, and dainty cheerleaders. None of that fit Natori's personality. She was thick, her natural hair color was white, and she would knock anyone's teeth loose for disrespecting her, her friends, or her family.

Natori felt that presence again, and she quickly looked out of the window only to see a blur dart somewhere behind one of trees.

"Ugh… Můj Bože…" Natori growled.

It evaded her again.

"Hey, someone's frustrated. I only hear you speak Czech when you're angry or when your dad's around. I don't see Akiko's muscular ass anywhere, so it must the latter. What's up?"

Natori smiled a bit and looked to Connor, her best friend. They had been friends since the 1st grade. They had stopped being friends for a while during middle school, but they had reconciled at the end of ninth grade. He wore a black muscle shirt and jeans with black biker boots. He was also the school's best quarterback, making him one of the most popular guys in school. Connor was the jack of all trades, his jet black hair dyed blue at the bangs contrasted nicely against his tall and broad form. His tanned skin was earned from the hard days of football practice in the hot sun. His status was the only reason why Natori was known around the school. His eyes were sapphire, making it easy for girls to get lost in his gaze. Natori however, was an exception; she viewed Connor more so as a brother. Her personality was why they got along so well. His calm, cool demeanor paired with her fiery, hot-tempered nature made them a great pair of friends.

Conner smiled as he reached forward and patted her head affectionately as a big brother would. Her father did it a lot, and if Natori had brothers, he was sure that they would too. It calmed her, and made it easier for her to open up about the reason for her current aggravated look.

Natori smiled and brushed his hand aside. "I'm fine Connor; it's just that I think I'm going to fail this final exam."

It wasn't a total lie, Natori was actually worried about failing and not graduating, it just wasn't the biggest cause to her frustration.

"No you're not, just study and I'm sure you'll pull out a seventy-one somewhere in there. Hey, if you work extra hard you may even pull a seventy-two! That'd be a first for this class!"

"Shut the hell up!" Natori shot back at him, sighing when he laughed hysterically.

Mr. Stark put his book down to lecture them about their behavior once again, but the sound of the bell deflated his speech. Natori quickly stood and gathered her things, rushing out of the classroom with Connor right behind her. The two took a deep breath of fresh musky air and let out a breath of relief. They were lucky the bell had sounded at that moment, or Mr. Stark would have talked their ears off until the bell rang. Natori hated being nagged about something she wouldn't stop doing.

"You'd think after the many lectures he's given us he'd realize that they don't work." Connor sighed.

Natori smiled, but said nothing in response.

"Tori are you alright? You don't think I've noticed, but you've really been on edge all day. Do I need to stop the cheerleaders while they're ahead again? I don't think anybody's forgotten about last year when you slammed that guy's head into the lockers."

"I'm fine Connor, just tired is all."

Connor didn't buy it at all. He had been Natori's best friend since 1st grade, he knew her better than anyone. He also knew that if Natori didn't tell him the truth now, she would later, so he didn't dwell on it for long.

"If you're that tired then just go home. I'll cover for you. Hell, I should at least cover for you once after all the times you've covered for me." Connor smiled.

"Really!?" Natori exclaimed, hugging him tightly. "Oh thank you, thank you, thank you!!!"

Connor gasped, laughing painfully. "Uh… You're short Tori, not weak! Let go before you rupture my spleen!"

"Oh! Sorry… Forgot!" Natori exclaimed, rubbing her neck with an awkward laugh.

Connor smiled endearingly. "Go home you adorably awkward thing you."

Natori laughed as she headed down the hall towards the double doors that would grant her freedom. It was the final two weeks before graduation, so Natori didn't care at all about attendance. All the seniors had to do was finish their final exams that were on different days than the underclassmen and they would technically be done with school. Sighing, she walked out of the school as quickly but quietly as possible, and then raced down to the student parking lot where her blue and black Mercedes-Benz was waiting. Upon reaching her beloved Macy, she pulled out her keys and pressed the unlock button.
Freedom was within her grasp.

"Hey! Seniors aren't to be dismissed for another two hours!" A voice yelled.

Natori paled and looked up into the ice green eyes of Richmond Academy's strictest administrator, Mrs. Brandshaw.

Mrs. Brandshaw was a tall, middle-aged woman with graying blonde hair tied into a ponytail. She was notorious for putting students in ISS for an indefinite amount of time.

One word to the principle from her would send even the most straight-laced students home for at least two weeks. Today she was clad in a blue dress suit with low-heeled sandals.

'The strictest female administrator of 2015 starter pack' as Natori jokingly referred to it.

Shit! Natori inwardly exclaimed. Thinking fast, she leaned over her car.

Mrs. Brandshaw wrinkled her brow worriedly. "Miss Sukimori are you ill?" she asked, stopping her detention ready stride.

Natori covered her mouth as if she were about to throw up. "Yes… Unfortunately… I-I'm so s-sorry… I-I asked C-Connor t-to-

"Shh… its ok don't use your strength, just go on home ok?"

Natori nodded wordlessly and slowly got into her car as if she were trying to avoid throwing up. She put the car in reverse and slowly pulled out of the driveway to make sure that Mrs. Brandshaw didn't suspect her to have faked being sick, even though that was exactly what had just transpired. Natori could always get away with misconducts with Mrs. Brandshaw. Unlike the other students, Natori appealed to the mother within the administrator. It was a well-known fact that Natori's mom wasn't in her life. In fact, she couldn't even recall her face. Her father had told her that her mother had realized that she was in love with someone else, calling off their marriage to be with her lover and leaving them both behind. Natori gripped the stirring wheel.

Neglectful skank.

"Macy, call *Otec*." Natori commanded.

Natori's Mercedes named Macy, called *Otec*.

Beep… Beep…

Beep… Beep…

Beep-

"This is Akiko Sukimori." A deep voice picked up.

"Hiya daddy!" Natori exclaimed, her face lighting up at the sound of her father's voice.

"Hey baby-girl, what's up?" Akiko asked.

"Nothing much, on my way home. What about you?"

"... On your way home? They didn't release seniors early... You finally asked Connor to cover for you then snuck to your car. You then got caught by Mrs. Brandshaw but you faked being sick so she let you go. How close am I?" Akiko guessed.

"Right on the money! You know me so well!" Natori gushed.

Akiko sighed. *"You've got two weeks left. When I was in high school I stopped caring about attendance two months before my graduation."*

Natori laughed. "Dad that's not good! But at least you graduated! So how's being a teacher at that special school?"

"Fun actually, I feel free here. The students are a lot more mature than the average student. The air is better, much more calming auras around here."

Natori wrinkled her brow. "Where are you? I wanna transfer there!"

"Natori you've got two weeks left, endure."

"Ugh! Alright." Natori sighed.

Akiko chuckled. *"Cheer up muffin. School just got out. I'll meet you home ok?"*

"Alright, bye *Otec.*"

"Zbohom Láska." Akiko replied.

The call ended, and Natori stopped at the light. Sighing, she waited for the light to turn green. She could never catch a green light in the city; she swore she caught every red light in existence on her way home from school. It was like a last chance attempt to sway her into going back. The sickening feeling of being watched rose again, but it was stronger than before, as if the thing watching her was in close proximity. Natori looked out of her car window. She looked out of the passenger window and checked all three back windows.

Nothing.

"Damn…" Natori hissed, looking to see that the light had turned green.

Driving on, she couldn't shake the feeling of someone following her. It had been watching her all day, and she could never pinpoint its exact location. Her nerves were fried, and her heart dropped when she somehow felt it closing in. She could almost feel the imposter's hands reaching out to grab her from her car, and she knew that if she were to be caught, no one would notice it.

Natori quickly sent a 'get home quick' text to her father and floored the gas petal. The car lurched forward, and she felt instincts that she had never felt before kick in. Her eyes sharpened, and her hands moved on their own as she sped to her cozy little home at the end of the neighborhood she turned on. Natori could feel something chasing her as she took various turns to shake off her possible kidnapper. Her father's 2015 blue Altima was in the driveway. She pulled up beside his car hurriedly. Turning off the engine, Natori jumped out of her car and rushed into her house. Leaning against the door, Natori's eyes lost their adrenaline vision.

Akiko rushed into the entryway of his home. His sapphire hair fell over his shoulder and emerald eyes scrutinized his daughter, assessing the situation. When he read her text his heart had sank into his feet. Natori had never sent him a text like that before. Of course she wanted to know how far he was from their home, but never 'get home quick'. She was leaning against the door, panting as tears rushed down her flushed cheeks. Her eyes were wide in fear. He had driven home straight from work, and had not changed out of his white dress shirt, nor did he loosen his purple tie. His black dress shoes were still on his feet as he had been pacing his living room worriedly, waiting on

Natori's arrival. He approached her slowly, knowing Natori's first instinct was to fight when she was afraid.

"Tori...? It's your father... Come here little one... It's alright, you're safe now..."

Natori launched herself into Akiko's arms, shaking as she tried with all of her natural born might not to sob. She failed, and clutched him as she sobbed pitifully into his shirt. Akiko held his daughter tightly, cradling her against him as any father would when their child was in distress.

"Hush... Hush Zlatíčko... Tell me what's wrong."

"Someone's following me! I-I felt eyes on me all day! A-and when I was driving it closed in! I thought I was about to be kidnapped!!" Natori exclaimed frantically, clutching onto Akiko tighter.

Akiko tightened his grip and scratched her scalp gently, knowing it gave her comfort. His eyes narrowed. He knew his daughter, and Natori wasn't one to back down from anything. It was unusual for her to be so frightened that she would cling to him as if he were her lifeline. Granted, she was a daddy's girl, and required his attention often, but never had she clung to him in terror. He rested his chin on the crown of her head.

"It's ok baby, I'll take care of it." Akiko told her, his voice firm and determined to protect his child.

Natori nodded, but she didn't let go. Akiko held her to him tightly without restraint. She was tough, his daughter. But she was still a girl, and the prospect of being kidnapped scared her. Hell, it scared him. Natori felt as if a barrier was protecting her. She could no longer feel the presence, and all she felt was Akiko hugging her protectively. Her breathing slowed, and Akiko smiled when he felt her full weight against him. Her breathing slowed to a relaxed lightness, and he knew she was asleep. He picked her up and carried her upstairs. Natori had a long day, and he knew it wasn't just all day that she had been feeling someone watching her. If that were the case it wouldn't have left her so terrified. She would have had to have felt this for a while now. She had to have been on edge for a while, and the adrenaline rush had tired her out. Akiko walked into his own room and placed her in his bed after removing her shoes. As a child, Natori would often crawl into his bed at night, and that tendency never left. He knew that she would rather be in his room instead of hers, his scent was all around, and she would take comfort in that fact. Upon leaving the room and closing the door, Akiko pulled out his cellphone and walked down the stairs into the kitchen. Dialing a number, he waited and a voice picked up on the first ring.

"Hey Buzzkill what's up?"

"Idiot… Give *Starší* back his phone Blake."

"Oh you don't want to talk to your big brother?"

"I don't consider idiots as family." Akiko sighed.

"… Starší! Come get your phone! It's Buzzkill!"

"Why the hell do you have my phone anyway!?" An angry voice in the background carried over.

"I was playing a game." Blake replied nonchalantly as someone took the phone.

"Ugh… Go annoy your dad."

"Alright!"

Retreating footsteps carried over, and the phone's owner sighed before putting the phone to his ear.

"Hey Akiko."

"Pyro, Natori's awakening…"

Pyro choked on air. *"How do you know?"*

"She's noticed Dawson's presence, and her aura was just dissipating when I rushed into the entryway earlier. She thought she was in danger and her powers activated slightly."

Pyro sighed. *"Alright, give me some time to get everything ready. Have you told her the truth?"*

Akiko lowered his head. "No… Do you think they're still searching for her?"

"Yes, until she awakens, they will not be able to locate her. But once she does..."

"We would have to keep her protected..."

"Exactly." Pyro stated matter-of-factly.

Akiko sighed. *"Starší..."*

"I know Akiko. But she's becoming a powerful warrior. Even more so than the average being because of her mother... I'll teach her personally, and we all will protect her. Her memories will also begin to return, so start explaining things. Preferably before she starts to notice any of the more drastic changes."

"I know... But Tori is stubborn, and no matter how drastic the changes are, she won't listen to reason. She's headstrong, and once she gets something in her head she won't change her stance. In her mind, she is a normal girl, and she won't listen to any revelation that contradicts that."

Akiko could hear the smile in Pyro's voice. *"I know... Just like her father."*

Akiko smiled. "I will *try* to explain everything to her. You get everything ready, and when she awakens, we will train her in using her powers. I already taught her hand-to-hand combat as well as weaponry. That's why she doesn't scare easy."

"... Please don't tell me we have the female version of Akiko on our hands."

"Of course you do."

"Můj Bože... I'll inform the nurse."

Akiko laughed and ended the call. He then sighed.

His little girl was awakening.

A day he both dreaded and awaited.

Chapter 2

"Memories are the hardest to stifle…"

"Oh she's a beauty!" A deep voice complimented.

"Thank you dĕdeček. She looks so much like you that I wouldn't be surprised if she turned out to be a triplet born late. Right Metri?"

Natori was sitting on her father's lap. Her white pig tails complimented her kid face, and her eyes held an innocence that she wished she still held in the present. She was wearing a white frilly dress with a purple ribbon tied around her and created a big bow in the back. Nine men surrounded her, and each man, including her father, sported a strange onyx rose on their left cheek, and black designs traced from their wrists to their shoulders. She could tell by their voices that they were men, but she couldn't see their faces clearly. As if there was a barrier shielding her vision. All she could see was her father's face and the markings each man sported.

Metri, whoever that was, laughed. "Yeah, I wouldn't be surprised if she acted like Roro too."

She heard their laughter, but she herself smiled when she saw Akiko hug her lovingly. Akiko seemed to be so familiar with these men, as if they were distant relatives. But Natori had no clue as to who they were. She still couldn't see their faces, but the markings were so clear and bold that it was the only thing she could focus on as the memory played out.

Natori shot up in bed, a light sheen of sweat covering her face. Grumbling, she looked to the alarm next to Akiko's bed. It read 5:30pm. That couldn't be right; she got home around 12:45pm, so that would mean that she had slept 15 minutes shy of 5 hours straight. Natori was never one to take long naps. 15 minutes, 20 at most. But the length of sleep was the least of her concerns. What was with that dream she was having just now? It felt so real, and her dream self was calling it a memory, but she didn't remember anything like that. What were those strange markings they all bore? She somehow knew that they weren't tattoos, and even her father bore them.

Natori slid out of bed and stretched her arms. She felt a dull jolt in her lower back, and she turned as Akiko opened the door. He wrinkled his brow when he noticed her standing there. He had finally traded his work clothes for a green muscle shirt and black shorts. His hair was in a ponytail and his shirt looked damp, which meant that he had just finished his third and final workout for the day. Akiko was a muscle head, and insisted that he hit the gym before work in the morning, during his hour break, and in the evenings when Natori was home. They had a gym built in their house, and she and Akiko would usually work out around this time. But she had slept through her workout.

"Are you just now waking up?" Akiko asked her.

"Yeah… I guess I was just tired." Natori replied, looking away.

Akiko noticed her lack of speech as he took a drink of his water bottle. "Something wrong honey?"

Natori sat down on the bed with a sigh, running a hand through her hair. "… I had a dream… But it was real. Well, it felt real. I was younger, and there were about eight men surrounding me, nine including you… And it was like I was meeting them all for the first time… But I couldn't see their faces; all I saw were these… Markings… They were strange… But beautiful… And my dream self called it a

16

memory… But I don't remember any of that actually happening… A cloaked memory perhaps?"

Akiko laughed, and Natori wrinkled her brow. She was used to him laughing at her dreams, but his laugh this time was different. Almost as if… He was nervous.

"Dad? Why are you so nervous? It was just a dream…"

Akiko nodded and crossed his arms, strolling over and sitting down on the bed beside Natori. He ruffled her hair playfully, making Natori laugh and shake his hand off of her hair. He was a teacher, and he knew that she would believe anything he told her as long as it fit with her own mindset.

"Your body isn't used to sleeping so long, that's why you had that dream. It's just a bodily alarm your body set up as a sure way to wake you."

Natori thought about it. "Hm… That sounds about right."

Natori suddenly turned towards the door with a blank look on her face.

Akiko grew worried. "Tori?"

"The door's about to ring…"

Just then, the doorbell did indeed ring. Akiko looked over to Natori, and then stood. He figured something like this would be the first sign he would receive. Natori also stood to her feet and followed Akiko out of his room and down the stairs towards the front door. How did she know that the door bell was about to ring?

Weird.

Akiko put his hand to the door, and then stopped. Natori showed signs of psychic abilities, and even as a just budding seed, they were strong. He decided to test her to see just how far she could see.

"Natori? Who is at the door? And why have they come?" He asked, already knowing the answer.

Natori wrinkled her brow. "How should I—" a face flashed before her eyes—"It's Connor, and he is here to bring my school work…"

Akiko nodded, and then opened the door. He was face to face with Connor, as Natori had predicted.

"Dobrý den Mr. Sukimori! I'm just here to bring Natori's school work."

Akiko smiled, his pride at the fact that Natori had successfully predicted both the person and their intentions overflowing from his chest. *"Dobrý den* Connor, come on in."

Connor walked into the house as Akiko closed the door. He looked up and smiled at Natori.

"Hey Tori… You ok? You look like you're going to be sick for real."

Natori had gone five shades of green, her tanned skin even discoloring slightly to show it. She shook her head and raced back up the stairs holding onto her stomach for dear life. Bursting into the bathroom, she hurriedly opened the toilet seat and emptied her stomach acid into the toilet. She hadn't eaten at all that day and her accurate predictions made her sick with fear. She groaned as she did this, throwing up plain stomach acid was a painful experience. Akiko and Connor had quickly followed her, and Akiko opened the door and both witnessed Natori on her knees, leaning over the toilet. Tears streaked down her cheeks, and Akiko knew that she was truly frightened. She now noticed that something was happening to her.

Akiko sighed. Now was as good a time as any to tell her. "Natori… There is something that we need to discuss."

Natori shook her head as she stood. She didn't want to hear anything anyone had to say about anything. She walked out of the bathroom and into her own room, closing the door and sinking onto the floor against the frame.

Akiko sighed again. "Connor, I need you to come back later. This conversation must be had alone. I'm sorry you came all of this way for nothing."

Connor nodded and smiled. "Don't worry about it. I'll be back later on today."

With that, Connor let himself out. He wondered if Akiko and Natori had gotten into an argument before his arrival. They didn't usually fight, seeing as how they were all each other had and both parties knew that. Maybe Natori was actually sick and Akiko had to talk her out of being stubborn and bearing it as he usually had to. Natori was headstrong, and often insisted that she was fine until the point where she nearly killed herself trying to carry on throughout the day with a fever or whatever. There were plenty of times where Connor had to call Akiko because his daughter had fainted, her body having shut down to prevent farther harm.

Akiko knocked on Natori's door. "*Zlatíčko*, please open the door. I know you're scared, and I know that you're starting to notice the changes taking place. Look, I know what's happening, and I need you to come out so that I can find the words to explain this to you…"

Natori opened the door and leaned against the door frame. Her eyes were red and puffy, and her face was slightly reddened. She had been crying.

Akiko hated to see her cry. "Aww… Come here." He told her, pulling her into his arms.

Natori sighed, letting her father soothe her panicked mind. He knew that while she was indeed tough, she was fragile at the same time. She took a deep breath, and finally felt her raging thoughts subside. She pulled back gratefully, and now that she had a clearer mind, she could ask the proper questions.

"Ok, tell me what's going on."

Akiko nodded. He led Natori from her room and down the stairs to the dining room. She sat down on one of the plush sofas, and he joined her. Akiko took her hands into his own and smiled as the fond memories of her childhood drifted through his mind. He remembered when Natori was just a pup, running around the house as if she owned the place. If she weren't sitting in front of him now, he wouldn't believe that she was a young woman now.

"Everyone is different, so let's start by you telling me what you've experienced so far ok?"

Natori nodded. "Well... As you know, I've been able to detect that strange presence watching me. I know it's always been there, but now I'm able to feel it. Now I'm having dreams that are too real to brush aside and I can predict things before they happen. That's pretty much it for now... Well if I think about it logically... The human body can detect when someone is watching them, and I knew Connor would be here sooner or later with my school work... I did look at the time when I woke up... I must have made a subconscious note that Connor would be here soon... I'm overreacting to perfectly logical incidents..."

There was a beep, and Natori looked down at her phone with a smile.

Akiko cursed. There she went with that psychoanalytical mindset of hers. "Tori I really think you should—"

"Dad it's Connor, he just invited me to a party. I gotta go get ready. Thanks for helping me figure things out!" Natori exclaimed happily as she hugged and kissed Akiko on the cheek.

Natori stood and rushed up the stairs, and Akiko growled. He knew better than to try and explain things to Natori. Her mind was so damn psychoanalytical that she could come up with logical explanations to the most humanly strange occurrences. Curse his teaching her to find the logic in everything.

"She's going to find out the hard way..." Akiko sighed.

He sent a text to Pyro explaining how their one-sided conversation went.

'Psychoanalytical mindset huh? Damn... She will have to find out the hard way then. It'll make her stronger than those who knew what to expect. If I recall correctly, my

youngest son had this same problem with a certain someone... Funny thing about those tables...'

"They always turn…" Akiko finished the quote with a smile.

Just then, Natori strolled down the stairs with a sigh. She had a weird feeling about this party, but she ignored it. Her father had told her that she spent too much time home and that she should get out more. All she did was go to school, study, workout, and spent time with Connor and Akiko. Connor had invited her to plenty of parties before, but she had rarely agreed due to the weird feeling she'd get about him not telling her the full details. Much like now, but she would ignore it and let Connor once again take pride in the fact that he dragged her to another party. She had also gotten at least an hour of workout in. She wouldn't feel right about skipping out on her gym time. She wore a black tank top and sweatpants, and she had a bag on her shoulder as she fiddled with her phone. Akiko had decided to turn on the TV, and was now watching one of his favorite shows.

"What time is the party?" Akiko asked.

"Around ten tonight since tomorrow is senior skip day, but Connor is coming to get me now so that we can go to this café. We're coming back two hours before the party to get ready." Natori replied, still fiddling with her phone.

"Alright *Láska*, have fun. Try not to body slam anyone."

Natori smiled as she opened the door. "No promises."

Natori walked out of the door and closed it. She immediately saw Connor sitting in his black porche that was parked in front of her yard.

"Hi Connor!" Natori exclaimed as she got into the passenger seat.

"Hey, ready to go?" He asked, putting the car in drive.

"Yeah," she wrinkled her brow. "What's wrong? You sound nervous."

21

Connor laughed as he pulled off. "Nervous? Who's nervous? I'm not nervous!"

Natori gave him a blank stare. "You used nervous three times in the same sentence."

The café wasn't far off, so they made it there quickly. Natori waited until they were sitting under an umbrella outside to let her eyes narrow. She knew it. "What aren't you telling me?"

Connor rubbed his arm and looked away. He suddenly stared at Natori, mouth agape. He could have sworn that her eyes were sapphire, but it was gone as quickly as it had appeared.

Natori leaned back in her seat and crossed her arms. Looking up at the umbrella shielding them from the sun, she sighed. "Cassie is throwing the party isn't she?"

Connor laughed nervously. "A... Minor detail..."

Natori nodded, clearly angry. "Cassie... The jealous nuisance that tried to make my high school life hell because she thinks that I broke you guys up... The same girl who talked one of her boy toys into provoking me so that I would slam his head into the lockers and get suspended... The same girl who started that rumor about me saying that I had, had multiple dalliances... The same girl that I could make a ten-page list about the methods she has used to provoke me to violence which got me that lame nickname 'Bricks'... Is throwing a party that you invited me to."

Connor sighed. "She said that it was an ode to seniors party. She also said that all seniors are invited and that even seniors from other schools are coming... Just go with me Tori, as a parting kindness?"

Natori rolled her eyes. "Alright Connor, I'll go."

Connor released the breath he was holding in. "Thank you! Anyway, have you decided what you're wearing?"

"It depends on the theme. Anyway, I need to tell you something." Natori sighed.

Connor wrinkled his brow. "What is it?"

Natori shrugged. "Um… Well, today when I told you I was worried about failing… It wasn't a lie, but it wasn't the main reason why I was on edge."

Connor nodded. "I figured as much. So tell me the truth. What was bothering you?"

Natori told him the truth of the things that she had been experiencing. Connor listened to his friend attentively, wrinkling his brow when she finally told him what had actually been bothering her earlier that day in Algebra II. Now that she mentioned it, he had noticed that she had been on edge for a while now. She would turn quickly at the slightest movement, and she looked ready to defend herself at all times. At first he thought that she was just ready to rearrange some cheerleader's face, but now he knew that it was much more serious.

"Someone's been stalking you?"

Natori nodded.

"Tori, you should call the police. You could be in danger! Tori, I would be devastated if something happened to you!" Connor pleaded.

Natori laughed. "Connor, look who're you're talking to! I'll be just fine. Besides, *Otec* says he'll take care of it."

Connor wrinkled his brow. "Didn't someone end up dead the last time Akiko *took care* of something?"

Natori shrugged with a devious smirk. "Hm… I don't seem to remember. Anyway, the service here sucks."

"Bad. The waiter's not getting a tip."

Natori giggled just as their waitress came over to their table. She was a tall brunet with gray eyes, wearing the café uniform with an apron tied to her waist.

"Sorry for the wait, we're extremely busy today." She informed them with a sigh, taking out her pad and pencil.

Natori and Connor looked around to see the once empty patio full of people. They weren't there before, she knew because she had looked around when they first strolled inside.

Connor wrinkled his brow. "Hm. I didn't see these people when we first walked in."

"Neither did I…" Natori mused, not liking the situation.

Natori wrinkled her brow suddenly, rubbing at her eyes and then looking again. She was definitely seeing clearly. There were indeed people sitting at the tables, but the sense of complete dread that had hit her was enough to have her on edge.

And she was rightfully so.

"Connor… We need to leave…" She whispered.

"We just got here! Come on chill out."

Natori sighed and gazed at the people. They looked normal enough, conversing with their respective companion, but what Natori saw was far from normal. A black light engulfed each and every person in the patio excluding herself and Connor. A girl giggled and covered her mouth, but Natori saw that she had the face and chest of a skeleton. She wore the clothing of a female, and that was how Natori could determine her gender.

'Glamour… A light spell to conceal one's true identity from the human eye… But one as powerful as you can see it clear as day…'

The dread pooling around her stomach was immense, but something told her not to allow the disgust to show on her face. And so, she chose to ignore what she saw, and instead turned her eyes back to Connor. She took a deep breath to steady her nerves; somehow, she knew that they were secretly listening out for any signs of nervousness coming from her. If they detected any nervousness from her, they would attack them.

'When you're a spy within the enemy camp, it is imperative that you do not show them anything that will possibly unmask you. Should you ever find yourself in one of those situations, remain calm, do what needs to be done, and get out.'

She could hear her father's voice as clear as day.

"So, do you think Cassie's party will be fun since you're so graciously dragging me there?" Natori asked nonchalantly.

Connor pursed his lips. "Would I ever drag you to a party that wasn't fun?"

Natori simply pursed her own lips and crossed her arms.

Connor relented. "Alright, but this party will be awesome! I promise!"

Natori sighed. "Ok Connor," she checked the time. "We should leave now, two hours until the party starts and we gotta get ready. Theme?"

"Sexy goth world." Connor said as he stood to his feet.

Natori followed his lead, rolling her eyes with a smirk. "So… She wants a taste of our world?"

Connor smirked as they made their way out of the café. They had gotten into the car when he had a sudden thought. It had been bothering him since the day he had met Natori.

"Hey Tori, can I ask you something?"

Natori closed the passenger door. "Yeah what's up?"

"Your dad's real hair color is really blue?"

"Just like my real hair color is white." Natori told him plainly.

Connor didn't believe her. He knew her hair real hair color was white because he had seen her unshaved legs one cold winter morning. But he had never had any stone hard evidence that Akiko's actual hair color was blue. Then it was sapphire, not light blue.

"You got any proof?"

Natori sighed, and then shuddered. "Ha… He walks around naked."

Chapter 3

"Temptation is the sweetest illusion…"

Day turned to night, and the party got underway. Cassie had rented out an abandoned house in the neighborhood. The gray house was two stories, and it looked extra creepy at night. Two fog machines blocked out the sidewalk, and the porch was decorated with withered roses. Cobwebs adorned the columns holding up the roof, and alternative music was blasting from the speakers inside. The turnout was no doubt phenomenal, and this party had the potential to end all parties. Most of the guests were inside, dancing to the beat that assaulted their ears, not that they minded. Upon walking in, what was once the living room of the home was pitch black save a disco ball emitting black light and red, blue, and green lasers. The three light sources created just enough light to be able to tell who everyone was and what they were wearing.

Cassie strolled down the steps purposefully, a conceited smile on her face as she carried her red plastic cup. Her usually brown, curly hair was dyed jet black and straightened. Emerald eyes were lined with black eyeliner and smudged around the whole of her eyes, giving her the stereotypical goth raccoon effect. Her peach, slender form was hidden under a black half-shirt and skinny jeans with black thigh high boots. Thin lips were painted ruby, and smiled at the compliments she received. Cassie was the girl everyone dreamed to be. She was both the most popular, and desired girl in the entire school. She was captain of the cheerleading squad and surrounded by ditzy cheerleaders that were willing to do her every whim. Boys fell over themselves trying to get to her, and she was the reason for many fights between the male classmates.

"You look great Cassie!" A classmate exclaimed as she passed by.

"I know," she replied, flipping her new raven tresses. "It's a job looking like me."

Cassie reached the dancefloor and slapped fives with every senior she saw. She had even kissed some of the boys on their cheeks, just to tease. Her eyes locked on the door as Connor strolled in. His natural raven tresses were down to his shoulders, and his ends were dyed purple while his bangs were neon blue. It was his usual coloring, but normally Connor would have his hair tied back in a low ponytail. His tall, toned, sun-kissed form was clad in a white button up shirt that was unbuttoned at the end, showing off his toned stomach. Sapphire eyes were slightly lined with black eyeliner to make them pop. Black leather pants hugged his legs and spiked black boots covered his feet. Neon green lip rings decorated his full, snake bitten lips, and he smiled as if to say 'I do this every day.'

Cassie made her way over to him with a smirk. "You look great Connor… Makes me miss the days when you were mine."

Connor smirked. "Thanks… So do you."

Cassie looked around. "Where's Natori? When I asked you told me you would figure out a way to drag her here. What? Is she scared?"

Connor laughed. "She's walking in now. I thought you would have known by now that Tori doesn't back down."

Cassie followed Connor's gaze towards the door and crossed her arms. She would never understand why Connor was so infatuated with Natori. She wasn't popular, she was fat, and did nothing but fight and study. She was rowdy and uncivilized, not at all like the lady she should be. And she was definitely nothing like Cassie, she was the goddess of

Richmond high, and Natori was a disobedient peasant who deserved everything she did to her. Natori was the reason her and Connor had broken up, if she would have just kept her big mouth shut she would still have Connor, and Cassie would not only have the hottest boy in Richmond High, but all of the other side toys she wanted, and Connor wouldn't suspect a thing. But no, she just had to go and tell him, and even went so far as to show him proof! He had broken up with her at the end of freshmen year, and Cassie had vowed to make Natori's high school life absolute hell for embarrassing her.

Natori's usually straight hair was curled loosely over her shoulders. White eyeliner not only enhanced the cat shape of her eyes, but it also made the amethyst orbs pop seductively. Natori wore a matte purple corset with a matching metal-looking tutu. Black heeled boots covered her feet. Black lipstick decorated her full lips, as well as her signature lip rings, which were matte purple as well. Cassie growled; even she had to admit that Natori looked hot.

Natori walked over to Connor and gave him a hug, laughing with an awkward blush as he complimented her. It was obvious that Connor was head over heels for her, he had given Cassie the same look once upon a time. That was a time when Natori was an unknown, and she had hated Connor just as much as she hated her. Then why? Why would she help someone she hated?
Natori gave Cassie a once over, and admittedly she did look good, save the stereotypical raccoon eyes every Glam thought they wore. Natori had no reason to be jealous of any girl, and she happily gave props where props were due. The party was over-crowded, but it seemed fun nonetheless, perhaps Connor would be right for a change. Cassie still glared, but then she gave a plastic smile.

"Wow Tori, you look hot. I thought you might have been too thick in the hips for a tutu, and I really thought you would be entirely too busty to be able to fit a corset.

You might actually be able to stand a chance against me for a change." Cassie giggled.

Natori arched her brow. "Thanks, but no. No self-respecting Goth would be caught dead standing beside some raccoon-looking bitch who mistook Goth for being demonically possessed. And for your information unlike you, I'm fit, and when girls like me eat properly and workout for an exceptional amount of time our bodies form muscle, and the actual fatty tissue goes to where it needs to be. So I may be fat to you, but other people tell me that I'm curvy, or that my body is what their working toward. Nice party by the way, I might be actually impressed instead of unmoved by your other parties Connor has dragged me to. Thanks for inviting us!"

Connor snickered as he took hold of Natori's hand and led her away from a fuming Cassie and into the kitchen. He loved how ruthless Natori was, and the way she insulted those who thought themselves her better was a thing of beauty. Much like Natori herself.

"That was beautiful Tori! You want something to drink?" Connor asked, slapping fives with a fellow football player, who then hugged Natori as he passed by.

That was thing about being friends with Connor. She had also become good friends with the entire football team, and there were many days when her and her father would have cold water bottles waiting for them after practice or a game. Not long after her and Connor had rekindled their friendship freshmen year, she was approached by another football player when she had walked into the cafeteria on the first day of sophomore year. He had offered her a seat at their table, and she had looked over and saw Connor waving at her, and so she had accepted. They were actually really cool, and they all had bonded or whatever during that lunch session. Although she was indeed popular, she kept to herself, and only hung out with Connor. Parties and football games wasn't what she was interested in, and so she only went to a home game when Connor was playing, which was every home game. She was sure that he could hear her cheering him on whenever he ran the ball.

Natori hugged herself and looked around. She thought that she would be used to being around so many people by now, but she wasn't, she always had a feeling something bad was bound to happen with this many drunken high school students in one place. "No… This is more your scene than mine Con."

Connor smiled at the pet name and then shrugged. He grabbed a bottle of vodka and took a gulp from the bottle itself. "That is true. Go get to know people and dance, I'll be here getting drunk."

Natori smiled softly. "You are such a bad influence."

"Mhm. I love you too. How do you say that in Czech?"

"Miluji tě is 'I love you'. 'I love you too' is *Take tě Miluji."*

"Nice. Go have fun, if you come back and I'm not here keep dancing, Cassie will have most likely convinced my inebriated mind to go upstairs and have wild, drunken sex with her."

"Ew." Natori laughed, walking towards the living room where the dancefloor resided.

The lasers illuminated her skin in greens, reds, and blues. Natori made her way through the grinding bodies to the center of the floor. It was surprisingly less crowded there and she figured that she would be more comfortable dancing. Upon reaching the center of the dancefloor she smiled, throwing her hands into the air and rocking her hips to the beat. The beat was sensual in contrast to the actual words, and so she danced in a way that matched the beat. The stress of the day had melted away, and soon she had forgotten all about her mounting problems. A hand grabbed her arm and turned her around. Natori glared and went to tear into him verbally, but stopped short.

Wow.

His red hair stopped at his shoulders, and molten gold eyes looked her up and down appreciatively. He was tall and muscular, with peachy skin that was clad in a deep red fish tail vest and black skinny jeans with a silver chain attached to his front and back belt buckles, making the loose chain loop around his side. He wore black leather boots and his lips were full and decorated by gold spider bite lip rings on the left side. A gold ring adorned his right eyebrow as well.

"Hey." He smiled, his deep voice washing over Natori.

She smiled; even she had to admit that he was gorgeous. "Hi."

"I saw you dancing and had to come over and talk to you. I'm Shawn, you?"

"Natori. I've never seen you around Richmond before..."

Shawn smirked. "Of course not, I go to another school, but a senior nonetheless. A girl like you shouldn't be dancing by herself. Mind if I join you?"

"Not at all." Natori smirked.

Another beat started, it was wild and erratic, and Natori ruffled her hair and moved her hips to match the new wild beat. Shawn pulled her to him, and they moved completely in sync. She smiled as she moved against him, let her hands rub down her own body before moving them back up to the roof. Her lower back jolted more fiercely than ever before, but she paid it no mind. For the first time, she was actually having fun without Connor or her father. She turned to face Shawn and smirked deviously, wrapping her arms around his neck. It was like she was in a different universe, one where she could actually enjoy herself.

"You're a great dancer, I bet the boys pant after you like rabid dogs." Shawn told her, making Natori laugh.

"Spare me please. I don't give idiot boys at Richmond the time of day. Except for my friend Connor, but he's no idiot."

"I should be grateful then." Shawn smiled, letting his arms snake around her waist.

"Totally," Natori winked. "So, how do you know Cassie?" she asked to change the subject.

Shawn shrugged dismissively. "We hooked up a few times freshmen year. Nothing too serious."

Freshmen year? That couldn't be right. Connor and Cassie had dated from seventh grade to the whole of freshmen year, and they broke up on the last day of school that year. If what Shawn had just told her was true, and he'd no reason to lie to her, then that meant...

Natori growled furiously, pulling away from Shawn and clenching her fists. "That... Whore..."

"Cassie? She told me at the time that she was single."

"Well she wasn't." Natori deadpanned.

She moved further away from Shawn and stormed from the dancefloor entirely. Walking back into the kitchen, she found Connor and Cassie making out in one of the corners. Natori grimaced, and then walked over to them and snatched Connor away from her. It was a well-known fact that Connor lost the entirety of his mind when he became drunk, and Cassie, who wasn't nearly drunk, was taking advantage of that.

"Tori... Is was havings fums..." Connor slurred.

Natori turned on her heel and slapped Connor hard with the momentum of her turn. Opened palm, tensed hand, and the power of the wind all combined into one harsh strike across the cheek.

"Ow! Tori that hurt!" Connor exclaimed, now completely sober.

He was secretly grateful for her slap, because her knocking some sense into him was the fastest way to sober him up from the most drunken states. But she was strong, and her hands were heavy, so it stung something fierce.

"There's something you need to know."

Natori dragged Connor outside and to a more private part of the yard where his car was parked.

"What's the last thing you remember?" Natori asked.

"Cassie and I talking about getting back together. Well, it was more of a one-sided conversation because I don't want to get my heartbroken like freshmen year. She was telling me that she was willing to drop all of her boy toys for me. Why?"

Natori crossed her arms and looked away with narrowed eyes. Connor was a man of honor, and even if he didn't remember telling Cassie that they were an item again, if she told him that he would go along with it, such was his heart.

Connor wrinkled is brow suspiciously. "You know something don't you? Because I think I was really considering it. Freshmen year I had my suspicions, and you were the one that confirmed it. Don't let me consider this without giving me a way out beforehand."

"Yes Connor, I remember showing you pictures of her and one of her boy toys like you asked, and you were right of course, but there was another guy she was fooling around with behind your back."

Connor snorted and shook his head. "I knew she was lying when she said he was the only one... How did you find out about the other one?"

"I was dancing with him. His name is Shawn, red hair, gold eyes, weird aura but has a way of making you ignore it... Typical irresistible bad boy."

Connor's eyes sharpened, as they did when he was pissed. "Mhm. Take me to him."

Natori shook her head. "I don't feel like explaining to father as to why I need to bail you out of jail. I only told you because I had a feeling that she would try to sneak her way back into your drunk mind. You don't need her, and you deserve better. Let's go back inside and get our stuff so that we can go. Ok?"

Connor sighed, but nodded as he followed her back into the house. Cassie was of course surrounded by her friends, she smiled at Connor, who rolled his completely focused eyes with a snarl.

"Don't worry about her Con. We were here to have fun, and we did that, Mission accomplished." Natori sighed, running into Shawn.

"Hey, you left before we could have a true conversation. You seem interesting, I would love to know more about you." Shawn smiled.

Connor pulled Natori behind him, glaring hostilely at Shawn. "Back the hell off! She isn't interested in guys who help girlfriends cheat on their boyfriends."

Shawn smirked. "I take it you were Cassie's boyfriend freshmen year? Sorry man, I only just found about you. Guess you weren't relevant enough to stop her from coming on to me."

Natori was uncomfortable; she could feel the tension between Connor and Shawn growing, as was Connor's legendary temper and his likeliness to hit someone. Connor was both taller and broader than Shawn, and Natori grew more and more uncomfortable as the tension continued to thicken.

Connor smirked. "Hmph, and I guess you liked the taste of my dick too much to stop kissing her."

"Ok!" Natori interjected, stepping in between Connor and Shawn. "My friend and I have to go study for our exams tomorrow. It was nice to meet you for the first few minutes. Have a good night."

Shawn glared hostilely at a now smirking Connor before turning back to her. "See you around."

Natori nodded uncomfortably, hoping for Shawn's sake that he and Connor never crossed paths again. Connor was inhumanly strong; she had seen him spar with her father and lasted a lot longer than anyone else besides her ever had. Natori grabbed Connor's hand and led him away, and Connor sighed forcibly through his nose.

"I'd have whooped his ass had you not been here." He growled, allowing Natori to do so.

They didn't really take anything in there with them, and were only going back for their drinks. However, Natori knew that one more encounter like that and Connor would be escorted out of the party in handcuffs. That would damage his sports career, and she couldn't have that.

Connor pulled his hand free once they were outside. "I wouldn't hit anyone in your presence Tori, I respect you too much."

"I know, but his aura… Isn't good, and I can't ignore it anymore. Besides, you would sneak away from me and fight him. I know you too well."

As they moved toward the door, Shawn crossed his arms with a smirk. She was definitely the girl his clan was looking for. He could see the electric purple aura surrounding her as soon as she walked in. He wondered how much longer she had until she would awaken and become a beckon for all to see. The only reason why he could see her was because of his ability to detect auras from even slumbering beings. His clan often used him to track down slumbering creatures. But she didn't have long, too soon for his clan to take her before she awakened, and she was fit, so he knew that she would give them hell.

"Did I do good master?" A voice asked from behind him.

Shawn turned to Cassie with a smirk. "Yes pet, keep pushing her."

Cassie nodded and walked off, making Shawn chuckle to himself. Humans. They were so easily manipulated. Their minds were feeble; they couldn't even fully access one hundred percent of their brain without going insane. It was fun, and it made his job all the easier. Cassie had unknowingly been his puppet since freshmen year, coming to him to report any student that showed abnormal abilities.

36

He honestly had no idea about that Connor guy though, not that he really cared. He followed behind Cassie as she headed outside to do as she was commanded. He could tell that Natori was angry, she wanted to say something to him for insulting her friend, but she also didn't want to start a fight, so she took the higher road.

How noble.

"Natori!" A voice shouted as she and Connor made their way to his porche.

Natori took a deep, calming breath before turning around to see Cassie walking over.

"What!?" Natori asked hostilely, seething with both the new information and Connor's encounter with Shawn.

If Connor hadn't been close to hitting him she would have slapped some sense into Shawn herself, and Cassie was really pushing her luck, addressing her so casually as if they had always been friends. The jolt in her lower back was back, but duller than usual. Natori wrinkled her brow as her eyes caught the dark aura surrounding Cassie, mostly her head. Something was wrong with this situation, but Natori was honestly too angry to care about logic.

"Did you have fun dancing with my leftovers?" Cassie sneered.

This bitch was really asking for it now.

Natori's left cheek, arms and thighs began to burn dully. "Not as much as you did freshmen year."

Cassie flipped her hair. "So what of it?"

Natori's eyes narrowed furiously, and the burning sensation on her skin spread throughout her entire body. Some places were hotter than others, and she could swear she felt something burning onto her skin. Her temper was rising, and she took deep breaths and shook her trembling hands to try and calm down.

But she was her father's daughter, and as such the urge to knock her into next year steadily increased.

"Můj Bože... I'm going to slap the piss out of you... If I recall correctly, you were definitely dating Connor freshmen year!" Natori told her, her voice dangerously low and clipped.

"Yes," Cassie told her. "I was dating Connor... Until you stuck your nose in our relationship. I just don't understand why you would help someone you hated back then."

"Shows what you know you imbecile! Connor and I had been best friends since the 1st grade! We had an argument in middle school which caused us to stop being friends, but I never hated him! And even if I did, nobody deserves to be played by some slut! No matter how I feel, if I see someone getting cheated on I'm not going to stand by while that person makes them look stupid in front of the entire school! Especially if that person *asks* me to confirm their previous suspicions!"

Connor grabbed Natori's hand. "Let's just go Tori, don't let her pull you out of your character."

Natori squeezed Connor's hand, growling. Her body felt as if it was on fire, and yet she wasn't bothered by the heat at all. "I'll knock her across the yard Connor. She can pick on me, but I'll be damned if I let her make a fool out of you."

"What?" Cassie sneered. "You're his mom now? No wonder why he can't stand you. A drunk mind speaks a sober heart Y'know."

"And my name is Steven since we're lying and shit!" Connor spat, stepping up. "I never said that stop twisting my words. I said that I couldn't stand you but since I was tipsy I would still make out with you. I wasn't drunk enough to not remember at least that. If you're going to quote me quote me right. And no amount of begging will *ever* make me want to rekindle our relationship. You're not fooling me twice."

"Natori… Did you always have those tattoos?" A boy asked.

Natori didn't register his words.

Cassie giggled. "Please, you were never important to me. You were something to be used, and then tossed aside like the trash you are!"

Natori moved. Fast.

Before anyone knew what happened, Cassie had hit the ground a few feet away from Natori, and her lip was bleeding profusely. Natori trembled all over, and Connor grabbed her before she could rush over and deal Cassie another blow. Everyone knew that Natori didn't tolerate anyone talking to Connor that way, she had beaten up guys and girls that disrespected Connor. She was relentless, and everyone knew that she had learned how to fight from a man. It was why she was dubbed 'Bricks'.

"Did you like kissing my fist bitch!? Because you've been begging to do it for a while now!" Natori yelled, fighting against Connor to get to Cassie.

Connor grunted as Natori yanked him forward, and he had to catch himself before he fell. Natori was strong, and her strength made it hard for Connor to subdue her. As such, he had to use a combination of both restraint and persuasion.

"Tori!" Connor exclaimed, turning her around to face him. "Hey, it's alright…"

The adrenaline went to her head, and Natori gave Connor a pained look before her eyes rolled into the back of her skull. She fell against him, and he picked her up into his arms effortlessly. Placing her into his car, Connor got into the driver's seat and pulled out, leaving the party with an unconscious Natori in tow. Shawn witnessed the scene with a smile before going over to and helping Cassie off of the ground. Someone handed him a damp cloth and he began dabbing at the blood on her lip. Even he had winced when Natori landed that punch, and his acute hearing heard something pop. Natori could've broken Cassie's jaw if she wanted to, but settled on dislocating it instead. Even in a fit of rage she was able to control her strength.

Natori Sukimori would most definitely be their hardest target yet.

"Good job pet... It won't be long now." Shawn smirked, witnessing what Natori might describe as a *burning sensation*.

He had witnessed the markings of the Sukimori tribe tracing her skin, but unlike these humans, his mind wouldn't write it off as some trick of the light. He made sure Cassie would be alright before leaving the party as well.

It was time to report to his clan.

Chapter 4

"The veil of lies must someday part and reveal the truth…"

When Natori regained her consciousness, she found herself in her room. Akiko was sitting on her bed, leaning over and dipping a cloth in a bowl of water. He looked over and smiled when he saw her wakened state. He rung the cloth out and dabbed at her flushed face gently, and Natori smiled as she cupped the hand tending to her.

"I think I ruined Connor's night." Natori said, her smile turning sad.

Akiko sighed. "No, but he did say that something happened to your skin. Your cheeks are flushed as if you have a fever…"

Natori nodded. "My skin burned hotter the angrier I got, and I was livid," she yawned and turned towards Akiko, who listened attentively. "It was weird, I've never been that angry before. Now I don't feel very well, so I might have been getting sick. You know I *abhor* getting sick, so the subconscious knowledge of my body coming down with something must have contributed to my livid state."

Akiko smiled. "Don't worry, you're not going anywhere tomorrow and I called out of work. I know that you wanted to participate in Senior skip day but I don't think you should be in the same place as Cassie anymore. I can't have you catching murder charges. Anyway, I figured you'd be home late so I took my time in preparing dinner. You hungry?"

Natori nodded. "Starving. What's for dinner?"

"Chicken dumpling soup. I had a feeling you'd come home under the weather. Does that sound ok?"

"Yeah… I'm going to take a nap; my skin is heating up again."

Akiko smiled and stood, walking over to one of her nightstands where he had placed the ice-pack. He grabbed the bag and returned to his daughter's side, placing the cool bag on her forehead.

She smiled at him tiredly. "Thank you daddy."

"Mhm. I'm going to go check on dinner now."

Natori nodded and took a deep breath. She was still wearing the outfit she had on for the party. She got up with a pained groan and dragged herself out of the bed. She walked over to the door and opened it, knowing her father would hear her from the kitchen since it was beside the staircase.

"Daddy! You could have at least set out a change of clothes!" Natori yelled from her room, pretending to be irate.

"I don't wanna look at all of your woman products!" Akiko yelled back from the kitchen, his tone also playful.

"You walk around here naked!" Natori countered.

"I pay the mortgage and bills and that's only when you're not home! Not my fault you barge in here without calling!" Akiko yelled back.

Natori laughed with a fond roll of her eyes and shut the door once more. Her father could be so goofy sometimes, and it was refreshing from his usual reserved demeanor. Sometimes he would even lock himself in his room, and no matter how many times she called or knocked, he would not answer. She figured that he had inner dilemmas that he had to deal with on his own, and he didn't want to drag Natori into the enigma of his thoughts. She strolled into her bathroom and closed the door, removing her corset, tutu, lip rings, shoes, and makeup. She brushed her hair back to its bone straight texture and then prepared her shower. Natori yawned as she walked back into her main room and up to her dresser. She grabbed a pair of underwear and a bra, along with a purple tank top and black shorts.

Venturing back into her now steaming bathroom, Natori stripped out of her current undergarments and placed them in the hamper in the corner. She slipped into the shower, and sighed as the borderline hot water cascaded over her. Natori grabbed her orchid smelling shampoo and poured a generous amount onto her hand. She closed her eyes as she began to lather her wet hair and massage her scalp. Scenes from the party replayed in her head. She didn't feel bad about her fist connecting to Cassie's face, and she didn't feel bad about what Connor had said to Shawn about the situation with that toad.

Shawn.

Natori's lower back jolted at the thought of him. There was something sinister about him, and yet there was also something else that drew her to him. She saw the black aura surrounding him yes, but there was a white light that was closer than the black aura, almost as if he were being protected from evil. She shrugged, no matter what she had seen, he had still said something quite disrespectful to Connor and as his best friend, she could not, and would not let him get away with it.

Brushing the thought aside, Natori turned off the shower heads and exited the shower. She dried herself and then changed into her night clothes. She had been ringing out her hair with a towel before blow drying it completely dry when her hands suddenly stopped moving. Natori had glanced at the mirror briefly, but what she had seen froze her movements. Adorning her left cheek was a single onyx bud that looked to be blooming. Black designs traced up from her wrists to her shoulders, and down at her thighs were green vines with black buds attached to every interception of the vines.

'*Did you always have those tattoos?*'

She remembered the question as clear as day now.

These markings were the same markings she had seen adorning her own father and those men in her dreams. She smiled softly. She didn't know how, but somehow they made her feel whole, as if they completed a subconscious puzzle. Natori stared for a few more minutes, admiring the intricate designs before she finished toweling her hair. Pulling out the blow dryer from under her sink, she wondered what her father's reaction would be to the new additions upon her body.

Meanwhile…

"Ugh… Blake this is why I can barely stand speaking with you!" Akiko exclaimed as he finished stirring the soup.

"*You know you love me! But seriously… Her markings are showing? When did you see them?*"

"I saw them when I opened the door to her friend carrying her unconscious form. It's only a matter of moments…"

"*Anything of her mom?*" Blake asked.

Akiko sighed. "Her spiritual powers are profound; I can sense the combined powers of her mother and me living together in harmony within Natori. She will be a force to be reckoned with. I know it."

"*… You have a very roundabout way of describing how babies are made dude.*" Blake commented.

Akiko slapped the phone on the counter and counted to twenty, willing himself to quail his growing irate. His brother had a terrible habit and talent of pissing him off in ways he wasn't proud of.

"You know what? Give *Starší* back his phone. I'm done talking with you."

"Starší is still preparing for the new arrival, anyone else?"

"Otec."

"Haha! Wrong again! Otec's-"

"Blake I will come through this phone and bash your head into the nearest wall." Akiko told him tonelessly.

"Ok! Damn can't take a joke!" Blake exclaimed.

A few minutes of silence, and a light voice answered the phone.

"Hey big bro. Dad's helping grandfather. What's up?"

"Hey Alex," Akiko sighed, one hand rubbing his temples. "Is everything almost ready? It could happen at any moment."

"We heard. But yeah everything's almost ready. They're casting the last of the protection spells in her dorm. I hope she likes the set up. So her markings are showing? Like the rose is ready to bloom?"

"Yes, her abilities are manifesting at an extreme rate. She's developing fast and the Takahashi clan is closing in, I've already had to kill ten of them this past month. They know she's awakening, and even now before she truly awakens they can feel her powers."

A sigh came over the line.

"Damnit... I remember meeting her when she was just a toddler. Her hair was in cute little pigtails and she wore the most adorable white dress. She's not supposed to grow up so fast!!"

Akiko smiled fondly. "I know what you mean. But she's eighteen now, her powers would start to manifest like this... Especially someone in Natori's situation."

"My situation?" Natori asked as she came down the steps. Her hair was completely dry, and she was in her night clothes, obviously planning to sleep after eating.

Akiko slapped the phone to the counter, smiling brightly at his daughter. "The situation of your hunger sweetheart!

My boss is on the line checking on you. You must be starving after that party. The soup's ready so have at it!"

Natori wrinkled her brow, but shrugged and grabbed a bowl from the countertop. Akiko could hear his brother giggling on the phone. Natori fixed herself a plate of hearty soup and made her way up the steps. Once she was gone, Akiko walked into the living room and sat down. He sighed and put his phone back to his ear, turning on the TV in case she decided to listen to his conversation from her room.

Alex continued to giggle. *"You are too quick on your toes."*

"I know," Akiko sighed. "That's why you all looked at me when it came to lying."

"Hell yeah."

"Anyway-

A bloodcurdling scream frayed Akiko's nerves, and his blood ran cold. His stomach sank as if he had eaten lead. He could tell by Alex's gasp that he had heard it too.

"Go. The elders are on their way."

Natori's blood was on fire.

She had walked into her room with the intent of eating her bowl of soup before going to sleep. Her skin had suddenly become an inferno, and this time it had affected her greatly. She felt something burst within her, and her body stopped responding. The sudden pain made her scream and she was suddenly on the floor, convulsing violently. She could see, but could just barely make out shapes. She could feel her body changing. Sweat dripped down her forehead, and tears slid down to her ears due to gravity.

"Otec..." Natori choked, her breathing shallowing.

What was happening to her? Was she dying? The pain alone was enough to claim her life. Her vision began to darken.

No...

46

"Natori!" Akiko called as he burst into her room.

There she was, convulsing on her room floor, the light around her form burning brighter and brighter as her markings began to permanently mark her skin. He could hear his child's pained whimpers. Closing his eyes, he focused. His aura flared out and his eyes turned gold. A golden light shot from his outstretched hand and in an instant, Natori was concealed. Sukimori became vulnerable to attacks when awakening, and since Natori was now a beckon of power, any rival clan could enter her room and eliminate her while she wasn't able to defend herself. Akiko however would never let that happen, hence why he formed the barrier. It would hide her rising aura, and his power covering his child would automatically recognize her and attempt to dull the pain. Sometimes it worked, sometimes it didn't. He hoped that it worked however, because the pain alone was enough to kill her. A pair of light orbs flew in through Natori's window, and it morphed into humanoid shapes and vanished, revealing tall and muscular twin men.

Pyro and Demetrius Sukimori.

The two walked into the barrier and kneeled, assessing the situation. She was still in a great deal of pain, but it was lessened thanks to Akiko's experience with his younger brothers and quick thinking.

"You have done well Akiko, let us take over now." Pyro told him.

Akiko smiled slightly, Natori really was the feminine version of his grandfather.

"*Dědeček.* She's in so much pain…" Akiko whispered, his worry shining through and through.

Demetrius stood and walked over to Akiko, placing both hands on his shoulders comfortingly while Pyro was tending to the awakening young woman.

"Yes, but it is lessened thanks to you. Now, we must get her out of this realm before she is found and attacked. We cannot afford to lose the crown jewel of the Sukimori clan. She is essential to this."

Akiko nodded, watching as Pyro lifted Natori's still convulsing form gently into his broad arms. She shook violently against him but gritted her teeth, obviously trying not to make as much noise. Pyro smiled, as if she had something to prove. She gasped out in pain, and clutched onto Pyro helplessly. The pained eyes looking up at him, wide with fear broke his heart.

"Prosím! Pomozte mi... To bolí..." Natori whimpered, her voice trembling in agony.

Pyro kissed her sweat drenched forehead, knowing that she needed some form of comfort and reassurance.

"I know it hurts *Zlatíčko*... We're here to help."

Natori's vision blurred, and then blackened completely. Pyro clutched his great-granddaughter to him and shut his eyes tightly, growling. Of all of his power, he could not stop the pain his great-granddaughter was feeling at this moment.

He looked to Akiko. "Akiko you do understand, that you can no longer live this mundane life. I know that you left our realm thinking that the less she was around her family, the more of a chance she would have of not awakening. But obviously, your theory was wrong. You must come home immediately." Pyro told him, his tone leaving little choice.

Akiko nodded. "I understand *starší.*"

Pyro nodded to Demetrius, and the younger twin flexed his claws and sliced the air, creating a portal that would take them to their realm. The human realm was no longer a place for Natori, and as such the memory of every human that had ever crossed her path would be wiped clean of both her and Akiko, so no nonhuman would be able to track either of them. They walked through the portal, but not before Akiko grabbed Natori's iPod. She loved music, and he knew that she would be an absolute wreck without it. When he stepped into the portal, he watched it close. Akiko

48

looked to Natori's unconscious form sadly. He could no longer protect her from her destiny.

"I'm sorry *Láska…*" He said, looking towards the other side of the slowly opening portal.

Pyro looked down at the girl in his arms. Natori was still convulsing in her subconscious state, and her blank eyes were changing colors. She was obviously still in a great deal of pain, but they could do no more to help her. The pain of awakening was the first process of toughening her up. Though Pyro highly doubted that she needed much more toughening, considering the fact that she was Akiko's kid and was the spitting image of Pyro himself.

"I really do feel sorry for anyone who picks a fight with Natori. She was strong whilst she was slumbering, and she will only become stronger as she learns her abilities. Her body has a great deal of muscle built, she's small but I can feel the weight of her muscles. Akiko made sure that his baby girl would be ready for the life she will now have to live." Pyro commented.

"I agree," Demetrius said. "What shall we do? We cannot punish her."

Pyro shrugged. "We'll just have to keep her temper in check… Much like her father."

Akiko smirked. "Oh, her temper's going to get a lot worse. Mine did when I awakened. When will she begin training?"

"Hm. We will inform her of what has happened as soon as she wakes up. Considering who her mother is, she would have to train her in that nature of her powers. We can train her in our ways for the time being." Pyro replied.

"Could she be a hybrid?" Demetrius asked.

Pyro shook his head. "No. Her mom wasn't human, the Sukimori trait is dominant, but we all still receive some traits from our mothers. Since Natori's mom is who she is, it is safe to say that Natori will develop purification abilities. Added to our natural spiritual abilities, she will be a force to be reckoned with."

The portal opened fully to reveal a lush forest. It was nighttime, so all residents besides the trio would be sleeping. They stepped through the portal and it closed, leaving them surrounded by the black sky that was lit by the full harvest moon and bright stars. Akiko took a deep breath and released it with a smile. He truly loved being within the Sukimori realm, this was where he himself was raised, and where his family resided. He had missed them, and was truly happy to be home. They began their trek through the forest to the fortified sanctuary for supernatural beings. It was a large sized manor with powerful spells protecting the entire area. Humans saw nothing but a clearing, but others saw the wall blocking their view of the actual school. If malevolent forces tried to enter the school, they would first be pushed back as a warning, and if they tried to enter again, they would be burned to death, but the proper term for such a fate was purified.

Thanks to Akiko's wife, who first erected the barrier.

"She needs to be in our presence at all times so that her powers will be constantly quailed, so she will be placed in strictly Sukimori-taught classes. She'll also need an escort until she can navigate the school on her own... Jikiya will do. Her first class will be Dawson's, then yours Akiko, lunch is after your class, Alex and Ashten will be there... After lunch she'll train with Demetrius and me. Ok?"

Akiko nodded.

"Hmm... When she wakes, she may be extremely moody... Perhaps we should let her rest a while?" Demetrius suggested.

Pyro thought about it. "Hm... You are correct that is a possibility. She must meet everyone once again and we must explain everything... Her cloaked memories will no doubt begin to resurface, and she will become overwhelmed quite quickly. Mandatory three days' rest perhaps?"

Demetrius nodded. "That shall suffice," He stopped suddenly, on edge. "You feel that?" he asked, looking around with a low growl.

"Yeah… It feels like… We are being watched." Akiko told him, moving towards Pyro, who looked around slowly, tightening his grip on Natori.

Demetrius unsheathed a dagger and threw it with perfect precision. It flew into a tree. Their sensitive ears caught the yelp, the rustling of leaves and branches, and the eventual thud of something landing on the forest floor. The tension in the air lifted, and Demetrius narrowed his eyes.

"Stay here. I'll investigate."

"Be careful." Pyro told him immediately.

Demetrius smiled, and then stalked slowly towards the place where they had heard the thud. His aura flared as he disappeared behind nearby bushes, ready to defend himself if he were attacked. Pyro and Akiko felt the elements shift, just as Demetrius pulled a miniature body from the bushes. It was dead, the dagger having been embedded deep into its jugular. Demetrius tossed it, and it landed with another thump as it hit the ground in front of Pyro and Akiko.

"An imp?" Akiko questioned, surprised.

Demetrius made his way over so that the dead imp was within the triangular position the living beings formed.

"Yes, it is strange to find such creatures within the Sukimori realm is it not?"

Pyro had a hard look in his eyes. He looked down at Natori, she was no longer convulsing, but she was still very much unconscious. He could feel her aura rising and falling, and the light around her grew.

"… We need to get to the manor. Now."

Demetrius wrinkled his brow, but nodded, and they began sprinting to the protected manor. He, as well as Akiko could see the changes taking place within Natori, and the longer she was out in the open, the more dangerous it became. That imp was harmless, but Pyro still directed them to sprint. He knew when and when not to question the older twin. Pyro was tribe leader, and his word was law.

Something that he would harshly remind his subordinates of. Demetrius' position as his advisor granted him many privileges, but he knew that when Pyro got that look in his eyes, he knew something they did not, and his decisions were not to be questioned.

Chapter 5

"Once you awaken, you can never slumber again..."

"**S**he's beautiful father." He had told Akiko as they sat in the living room.

"I wish we didn't have to wait until she awakens to officially meet her." Another boy said, reaching over and cupping Natori's chubby cheek.

Natori had giggled. "Big brother! You are meeting me!"

He smiled, but it was sad. As if he knew something that she had yet to discover.

Three men sat in the living room of Akiko's home. Natori at the time was a five year little girl. She sat in their father's lap with a smile full of blissful innocence. Sitting in front of her were two boys. Both looked to be about eighteen years of age, but their aura revealed that they were much older. One boy was a more feminine version of their father, while the other one had long black hair and ruby eyes. Both were short and slender, but they were powerful she knew.

"She's going to be powerful. Especially since her mother is Chi—"

Natori awoke with a start. She sat up and immediately gripped her pounding head. That was what she got for sitting up so damn fast. When her blurred vision cleared, she looked around. It seemed that she was in some sort of infirmary. The walls were the traditional color of white, but that was the only part that was normal. Of course there were beds and curtains and the typical equipment one would see when in the infirmary. However, there were sofas and frames on the tables. It didn't even have the hospital smell, instead, there was an aroma of cinnamon, and the instead of the cool air, the room was toasty. But she didn't focus too much on her surroundings. She had absolutely no idea as to where she was, and she wasn't willing to wait and find out. The door opened and Natori lied back down and closed her eyes as nine men strolled into the room. She evened out her breathing, and forced her face to relax.

"We already know that you are awake. We're not here to harm you *Korunní klenot.*"

Natori sat back up at the term *'crown jewel'* and cautiously looked each man over. She sighed in relief when she saw that her own father stood among them. If he stood among them, then she knew that they truly did not wish her harm.

"Where am I?" she asked.

"OnyxRose academy." Akiko answered, walking over and sitting on the bed and cupping her cheek.

Natori felt the tears fill her eyes. "I… Thought that I was going to die… That I would leave my *otec* all alone…"

Akiko wiped the tears from her face with a smile. "No my daughter… We shall explain everything to you alright?"

Natori nodded, and then looked the rest of the men over.

"Father, who are these people?"

"Search through your memory." A man who looked to be the masculine version of her smiled.

Closing her eyes, Natori searched her memory for any recollection of the men standing before her. Yesterday's dream came to mind. She remembered it so profoundly because she had just gotten over her panic attack. She smiled bitterly at how her life had been flipped upside down in less than twenty-four hours.

"There's this thing… When I was younger… I was meeting some family…"

Her male counterpart smiled. "Yes, we remember that day quite clearly. You looked so adorable with your pigtails and your little dress… Time sure does fly…"

"Yes… I remember clearly, but I can't remember your names… Only blurred faces. I apologize."

"For what? We locked your memories away so that you would not remember until you were ready. I am Pyro Yoru Sukimori, leader of the Sukimori tribe, my nickname is RoRo."

Natori looked at him. "I remember hearing that… RoRo… Metri…"

The man that stood beside Pyro waved. "I am Demetrius Kaji Sukimori, head advisor. I also answer to Metri."

The two were exact copies of one another, and the only way you could tell the two apart was by looking at their hair and eyes. Pyro's hair was as white as her own, while Demetrius' hair was ruby. Both wore low ponytails to keep the thick tresses out of their eyes. Speaking of, Pyro's eyes were amethyst like her own, while Demetrius' eyes were as emerald as the gem itself. They were the same size in both weight and height, and they both possessed the same serious, yet mischievous aura. Their skin was tanned, an obvious trademark because everyone in the room possessed tanned skin. One thing was sure though, they were all gorgeous. She couldn't believe that she was the crown jewel when she herself was just average-looking. Natori felt like a human among Gods.

The man standing beside Demetrius was next. "I am Jikiya Ishi Sukimori. I am the oldest son of Pyro, I am also known as Kiya, but that name is only used by those of royal blood."

Jikiya was slightly shorter and smaller than the twins, but it was only slight. He too had ruby hair and emerald eyes, and she briefly wondered as to how he could be Pyro's son, when he looked so much like Demetrius. But she figured that since he was a twin, that he carried the genetics that would produce red hair and green eyes.

"So… Us?" Natori asked, referring to those currently in the room.

Jikiya nodded. "There are two others that shall join us shortly."

Two more..?...

Natori remembered her latest vision. "*Otec*… There is something I must ask you."

Akiko could tell by the tone of her voice that it was a serious question. A question so serious in fact that if he answered incorrectly that it would alter their relationship.

"What is it *dcera*?"

Natori looked confused and conflicted. She didn't know how to go about asking her question. She didn't want her father to lie to her, because then she wouldn't be able to trust him ever again.

"Ok… Um… Do I have a brother?" Natori asked him.

Akiko smiled. "Two actually. Do not worry; they are very excited to meet you again."

Natori bit her lip, still conflicted. She didn't understand how everyone could know about her, but her memory was wiped as soon as she found out about them. "How come I couldn't know about them?" She asked curiously, and immediately wished she hadn't.

Akiko had narrowed his eyes darkly, and his aura became charged with white hot rage. Natori flinched at the static as it spread to everyone in the room, as if they were sharing a painful memory. Her father had clenched his fist, and he had begun to tremble. One of his brothers noticed Akiko's state, and grabbed his hand comfortingly.

"Akiko... He's dead man..." He told him gently.

Akiko crossed his arms with a glare, and Natori lowered her head. She fiddled with her fingers nervously, not meaning to make everyone upset. She knew that particular question had struck a very sensitive nerve with all of them, and she felt terrible for asking such a horrible question.

"Is that supposed to make it alright!?" Akiko gritted through his teeth, glaring at his brother.

"No *malý bratr*, but it should give you a peace of mind. The dead cannot control the living, and they can no longer cause harm to those you care for." The brother replied soothingly.

Akiko nodded logically as the door opened. Two boys that looked about the same age as Natori walked into the room. They smiled at her brightly and occupied each side of her bed. One had emerald eyes and blue hair like her father. The other had unique black hair and red eyes. Both were tanned and slender built. A scene from one of her cloaked memories flashed in her mind, and her eyes widened in recognition.

"You two are my older brothers... Yukaro and Sebastian..." She murmured.

"Yes, hello *Mladší sestra*. I am Yukaro *Světlo* Sukimori, the oldest son of Akiko. I'm so glad that we can finally truly meet you!" He smiled.

Yukaro was the spitting image of Akiko, minus the built. He gazed at her lovingly, but Natori could see something else within him.

"My name is Sebastian *Rozkošnỳ* Sukimori, youngest son of Akiko. Are you feeling better?" Sebastian asked with a shy smile.

He reached up and cupped her cheek, and Natori sighed contently with a smile. Sebastian didn't look like anyone else in their family, but he was exceedingly beautiful nonetheless. Yukaro cupped Natori's other cheek, his brow wrinkling with worry.

Natori smiled. "There is still an ache, but it's better than before... Sorry if I worried you two... Can we finish the introductions? I'm excited about truly meeting my family."

Pyro chuckled, and then motioned towards the next relative.

A tall man stepped forward. He was slightly smaller and shorter than the previous men, but he was still very masculine. He had golden long hair in a ponytail, and his eyes were sapphire. He was tanned like the others, and he looked to be about twenty years old. Natori could tell that he was much older however, due to the sheer knowledge within his eyes.

"My name is Jeremiah Kuran Sukimori. I am the youngest son of Pyro Sukimori, who is your great grandfather; Metri is your great grand-uncle as you have no doubt already surmised. I am also referred to as Miah, and I am your grandfather. Either Jeremiah or Miah is fine, but I would prefer if you called me grandfather."

Natori nodded with a smile. "So... You'll tell me embarrassing stories of *Otec* when he was little won't you?"

Jeremiah smiled. "Of course I will."

"I am Dawson *Sensō* Sukimori. I am the oldest son of Jeremiah, and you may also call me *Krutỳ*."

Dawson was shorter than Jeremiah and had the same built as him, only slightly smaller. His hair was golden like Jeremiah's, but short like Jikiya's hair. His emerald eyes seemed to pierce through her very soul, and his aura spoke of immense strength and low tolerance.

Natori giggled. "You sound as if you have a low tolerance."

Dawson shrugged. "I tend to eliminate nuisances."

The next man had the same built as Dawson, and his hair was shaved into a Mohawk. He smiled, and Natori smiled back. He had an infectious smile and aura.

"Hiya there! I'm Blake *Láska* Sukimori. I'm the second oldest kid of Jeremiah. I'm often referred to as 'the fun one'! Sorry you got stuck with Buzzkill as a dad though. Sucks that God made you the punchline of a joke."

"Shut the hell up Blake!" Akiko exclaimed, smiling when he heard Natori laugh.

Blake's teal eyes shinned with kindness and overall joy, and she found herself laughing once more.

"Your aura is pure joy!"

Blake laughed and scratched the back of his neck. Natori's eyes narrowed suddenly.

"You are goofy... Like father... That means you're one of more dangerous ones..."

A gleam appeared in Blake's eyes then, and for a moment, the usual joyous personality he had dropped. *"Hm... You are of quick mind... A trait from your father no doubt... Much like him, you are able to see beyond sight. You would do well to hone your skills; fore you shall be a dangerous opponent... More so than Akiko."*

He smiled.

She smiled back.

Akiko stepped forward then. "I am Akiko Yoru Sukimori. I am the third oldest son of Jeremiah Sukimori. As you know these hands are Rated E for everybody so be careful who you hang out with around here."

Natori wrinkled her brow, and then smiled brightly. "That's adorable!!!"

"What? That I'll beat the snot out of students for messing with you?" Akiko asked.

"No! You have the same middle name as Pyro! You were technically named after Pyro! It's adorable!!" Natori gushed.

Akiko smiled proudly, while Pyro blushed.

The last two to introduce themselves were also twins. They were the shortest and smallest their brothers and father, but held a fire that was unmatched.

One stepped forward. "I'm Alex Sora Sukimori. I'm the older twin, and you can call me *Krásný* should you ever forget which one I am." He winked.

Alex had fierce emerald eyes, and though he was slender, Natori could tell that he was strong.

The younger twin waved. "Hey girlie! I'm Ashten Gokana Sukimori. Youngest twin and son of Jeremiah Sukimori! You can call me Ash, it's a pleasure to meet you and if someone messes with you and I find out about it I'm kicking ass."

Ashten's fierce sapphire eyes narrowed at the prospect of someone hurting their youngest. She was the only female in the history of the Sukimori tribe, and as such, they had to protect her. Not only from outside forces, but also from herself.

Natori nodded in agreement, and then rubbed her temples as she lay back down. This was a lot of information to process in one day. She sat up suddenly at the epiphany she just had. "That presence... It was you?" She asked Dawson.

"It was," Dawson confirmed. "It was my duty to ensure your safety at all times. Even when your abilities were locked your fierceness alone was enough to cause suspicion within enemy camps. They were closing in on you yesterday, and as such I raised my aura to redirect them to me, but unfortunately you were too close and felt both their presence, and my aura spiking. I apologize for scaring you."

Natori nodded. "Of course... It's alright. I never felt that you wanted to harm me, but it really was creeping me out. And then while I was driving I felt an aura that *did* want to harm me... I panicked. Anyway, when do I start my classes? What am I even learning?"

Pyro sat at the end of Natori's bed. "You shall learn the ways of the Sukimori tribe. Our history, how to use your abilities, and how we as a tribe operate and general things that comes with the territory of being Sukimori, more so you, since you are the first female of our tribe. You are a treasure, the crown jewel of the Sukimori tribe. There are things that will be expected of you, as your father established within you at a young age I have no doubt. And when there is nothing more to teach, you will be a force to be reckoned with."

Natori sighed. This was overwhelming. "Wow..."

Pyro chuckled. "It is borderline overwhelming I know, but what you need now is more rest, and time to think. When you awake it will be easier, and we'll explain more."

"Sleep? How am I to sleep when so much has been revealed to me!? I-I can't sleep! This is so exciting I can't even begin to explain the thrill rushing through me! Holy-

"Whoa!" Akiko exclaimed, laying her back down. "You need to rest honey. You actually woke up before your body could fully recover, which that in itself is an example of your strength. I promise you will learn all that you need to, but you must rest properly and let your body recover from the trauma it has experienced."

Natori nodded and closed her eyes. A wave of exhaustion hit her and she was asleep within seconds. Akiko nodded and caressed her hairline.

"Poor child... What the hell have I gotten her into?" Akiko asked himself, watching his daughter sleep.

Pyro crossed his arms. "This is her destiny Akiko. This is a revelation you can no longer deny nor can you attempt to diverge her from this particular path. God knows what he's doing Akiko, let Him take care of her."

Akiko sighed. "I know *starší*, I know…"

Natori made a noise of discomfort as she tossed and turned. She had never before experienced what her subconscious was currently subjecting her to. A series of pictures, passing through her dream self's sight in two second clips but yet… She could never un-see what she was witnessing. They were like paintings, telling the stories of each individual she had encountered before going to sleep. It showed her enough information to know them on a deeper level, but not enough to fully understand the being within the painting. Especially Yukaro, there was barely anything to show. She could feel her soul floating aimlessly through the galaxy, and she stared blankly as realization dawned on her.

She didn't know a thing about her own father.

Natori watched the tears that had gathered in her eyes float away, as there was no gravity to defy them where she was. Come to think of it, she didn't know how her soul traveled into the galaxy, she remembered being in the infirmary when she went to sleep.

'What the hell am I doing here?' she asked herself angrily.

Had she died after all?

"No Natori, you are not dead. You are exactly where you need to be." A voice answered her.

Natori sat up then, and realized that she was no longer floating aimlessly around the galaxy, but had landed in a different realm all together. The sky in this new area was purple, the lush sapphire grass covered the land, and there were flowers everywhere. The air was clean and crisp when she inhaled it, and she sighed appreciatively at the scene.

Earth was nowhere near this gorgeous.

This is magnificent… The peace here is unrivaled… She thought, looking up at the black stars in the sky.

"Yes," The voice answered once more, but closer. "Just like you."

Natori watched as a woman made her way towards her. There was a definite resemblance between them as far as feminine went, but that was about it. This woman had loosely curled orange hair and her golden eyes shone infinite wisdom. She wore a simple white dress, and adorning her head was a crown of onyx roses.

"Welcome, *moje dcera.*" She smiled lovingly.

Natori's eyes widened, and her body momentarily froze. This was her. The woman who had supposedly run off with another man soon after giving her life. Her father was right; the picture he had shown her was…

"M-mother!?"

Chapter 6

"The truth is often times stranger than fiction…"

The woman that stood before Natori nodded her head, smiling at her lovingly. Natori took a step back and shook her head in confusion. Here stood a woman that she had spent most of her life hating. The very same woman that had run off with her mystery lover soon after giving her life…

Was standing before her now.

"My name is Satori, and I've wanted to meet you for a very long time Natori." Satori told her, smiling.

Natori crossed her arms defensively. "Yeah, and I've wanted to meet you too… But why now? Father told me that you left us. I spent most of my life hating you… Why do you stand before me now? Why couldn't you help father raise me then? You do realize that to me, making yourself known means that you're ready to explain to me your indefinite absence from my childhood?"

Satori crossed her fingers in front of her and sighed. "Yes, I realize that I indeed have a lot to explain to you. Much like the rest of your family, you could not know of me until you were strong enough to be able to defend yourself against the foes that wish to do you harm. In fact, there are still some things that I cannot tell you, such as why you are so sought out."

"So being father's daughter isn't the only reason?" Natori asked.

Satori shook her head. "No, it is not. It is also because you are my daughter, and because of what you possess. There is so much that I wish to tell you... But you are not yet ready to hear what I truly have to say... Right now, know that I am your mother, and that I loved you so much, I sacrificed being a part of your life so that you could live... But I can no longer protect you..."

Natori nodded in understanding. It was just like her extended family on her father's side. She could know nothing of them until she had awoken, and realizing that it was the same for her mom, made her sad. How would she feel? If she were a mother that had to leave her daughter for the safety of her child? What life could she have possibly given her underneath such a profound shadow?

'Trap...'

'Hm?' Natori looked around; she could have sworn that she had just heard a voice.

'Trap... It's a trap... Use your sight... To unveil the light... The truth shrouded in lies...'

Natori looked to her mother for a long moment, and something peculiar caught her eye. Behind Satori was a tree, large like an oak tree that had seen a hundred years on earth. The leaves hung low, but it was the tree in its entirety that held her eyes. The tree's coloring was so out of place that she wondered as to how she hadn't noticed it before. The bark was brown, and the leaves were green but a sickly green, as if it had been surrounded in poison. It was a tree that had the same coloring as an earth tree, but it had been poisoned. Why would her mother summon her to a place that was potentially dangerous?

'Trap... Glamour...'

"What the hell…?"

The beauty of the realm morphed and burned away, leaving the complete opposite of what it once was. The sky was now black, and the other trees looked withered and poisoned like the large one she was under. The stars no longer glowed, and looked to be dull and dead as they hung limp in the sky.

"Mom… Why am I seeing this?" Natori asked as she looked to her mother, and froze in horror.

Her mother was no longer her mother, and standing in her place was a woman with the lower body of a snake. Her hair was wild, stringy, and black; and Natori knew that if she had been any closer, she would feel the effects of the sickly green aura surrounding her. Natori looked down at herself, noticing the electric pastel purple light that surrounded her. The snake woman moved, and Natori grunted as she was pinned to one of the other trees. The clawed hand that had clamped onto her neck squeezed, and Natori cried out as the claws dug into her skin.

The snake woman hissed. *"I don't know how you managed to lift my glamour… But it matters not... YOU WILL BE OURS!!!"*

Natori clamped her own hands around the one holding her against the tree. She didn't know how she managed to lift it either, but she knew one thing. She would be damned if she let some random snake thing with horrid breath subdue her. The burning started once more, but it was more controlled. Natori's eyes narrowed as she dug her nails into the scaled skin. A hot, purple light formed in her hands, and as her anger rose, so did the heat of the orb. Electricity began to emit from Natori's hands as well, and the snake woman began to scream.

"Let... Me... GO!!!!" Natori screamed angrily, and the light burst.

The scene blackened into nothing, and the last thing she heard was the woman's dying screams.

Natori sat up with a start, and she gripped her pounding head with a whine, regretting how fast she had sat up... Again.

"My... Head..." Natori groaned as she flopped back down.

The door opened, and twins Pyro and Demetrius entered her room. They had felt her aura rise suddenly, and they decided to check on her. Upon walking into the infirmary, they felt how light the air around the room was, and noted how exhausted and pained Natori looked. She grabbed her neck, and then looked over to them with a pained smile.

"Hey... I sat up too quick..." Natori groaned.

Pyro's eyes narrowed as he sat down on her bed. "Were you dreaming?"

Natori nodded. "I... Think so...? I was talking to my mom and then I noticed this huge tree that wasn't there before and then my mother turned into this hideous snake thing and pinned me against a tree. She said that she didn't know how I managed to lift her glamour but it didn't matter because I would be theirs..."

Pyro and Demetrius shared a look.

"And what did you do?" Demetrius asked, taking up the space on the other side of the bed.

Natori shrugged. "I told her to let me go and this electric purple light burst from my hands... Last thing I heard before waking up was her dying scream... Was that supposed to mean something?"

Demetrius shrugged. "How do you feel?"

68

"Like Dwayne Johnson punched me in the face." Natori replied.

Pyro chuckled. "I figured. It is time to enroll you into the school. I have your uniform here."

Natori sat up and groaned, but nodded her head. Her head felt like a log. Demetrius cupped her cheeks, and a soft blue light emitted from his hands. Her headache was gone, and any trace of grogginess vanished into nothing. Demetrius smiled and the light diminished, and Natori's eyes widened. Her headache was completely gone! And she didn't feel any of the grogginess she should've felt. She launched herself into Demetrius' arms, nuzzling his chest as he chuckled at her way of thanking him.

"You're welcome Tori."

Natori pulled back and yawned, stretching her unused muscles.

"The bathroom is through that door, don't take too long." Pyro told her as he handed the passing girl her uniform.

"Got it!" Natori replied as she walked into the bathroom and closed the door.

The bathroom was perfectly equipped for her to perform her daily routine of washing and getting herself ready, and she used it to her advantage as she prepared for her first day of classes. When she walked out, instead of the pajamas she was in while she was unconscious, Natori wore a golden collared T-shirt with a pale blue V-neck vest. The white cheerleader skirt reached her thighs. White and gold-trimmed socks reached her mid-thighs and simple white tennis shoes covered her feet. Her hair was combed and brushed, and was tied into a ponytail by a pale blue ribbon.

"Alright, I'm ready." Natori sighed, clearly not liking the less than dark colors.

Pyro smirked. "Earn your place and you won't be wearing those colors long."

"Awwww! You look so cute!!!" Demetrius gushed, walking over to her with something wrapped in a purple cloth.

Natori sighed, but smiled, completely used to her father gushing over every milestone she had ever crossed.

"What's that?" She asked, noticing the silk.

"This is just something your father used to carry around. I thought since you two acted so much alike, that you would be delighted to carry it too." Demetrius smiled, holding it out for her.

Natori's eyes glittered at the offer, and ever so slowly, she unwrapped the cloth.

Her eyes widened. "What!? You guys allowed *my dad* to carry *this!?*"

Pyro chuckled. "Yes. You, as well as your father, are royalty, and as such you are allowed certain privileges, like carrying this."

It was a sword. The handle was black and the blade was silver. She could tell that her father took great care of this sword, as he did all of the weapons he possessed. The very first thing he had taught her was the proper way to clean any weapon she possessed. The two of them would spend hours together, meticulously cleaning and polishing each and every weapon that was stored in their room.
Yes, father had even given his cherished weapons their very own room.

Natori wrinkled her brow. It was a beautiful sword no doubt, but every single one of her father's weapons was beautifully designed, so she couldn't imagine a time when he would carry something so… Plain.

Ew.

Demetrius smirked. "I know what you're thinking, and no, Akiko would *never* carry something so plain. He always was more interested in… *Creativity*. Instead of taking the sword to a forger and spending his money having modifications made on the sword itself… He used something like a prayer, a prayer he would recite to make it his. Death and life are in the power of the tongue, and which you use you shall reap the fruit thereof. Depending on what you say, the sword will form in the likeness of the type of prayer you speak. This sword will become a part of you, and you will become a part of each wielder before you. A piece of your soul will be fused into this blade. Recite your prayer, and whenever you wish to wield this blade, it will morph as soon as you touch it, fore your soul will react to it."

Natori nodded logically as she grabbed the handle. "Oh cool… I notice you quoted a bible verse…"

Demetrius nodded. "God is real."

"How do you know?" Natori asked.

Demetrius smiled, but it wasn't the happy smile he wore a few minutes ago. It was sad, as if he were remembering a turning point in his life that changed the way he thought about things. "That's… Another story for another day… For now, let's see what you come up with."

Natori looked at him for a moment, but she couldn't feel out his emotions. She looked to Pyro, who stared at his younger twin worriedly. They looked as if they had been through something traumatic, and she vaguely felt the dull jolt in her back again. Something dark flinted through their eyes, but it was gone as quick as it had appeared. She wanted to ask them about it, but something told her that neither brother was ready to talk about that particular memory. Instead, she looked to the plain sword she held. A mantra would bring it to life, and depending on what she said, the sword would contort to her words. If so, then she would do something never done before, something that was most likely forbidden among angelic creatures such as Sukimori. Natori sighed dejectedly as she decided that there was nothing she could do to lighten her great grand-uncle's mood. She turned her attention back to her new sword. She ran her hand gently over the blade itself, noting the meticulous sharpness and shine. It might have looked plain, but father had taken care of this sword like he did his other weapons.

"What was father's name for this sword?" Natori asked curiously, looking to the older twins.

Pyro looked to her and smiled gently. "He called it Kuran Kaji."

Natori smiled. "Dark flame... Nice... I hope it likes what I name it... Whatever that is."

"The name will come to you. Have you thought of a mantra?" Demetrius asked, his mood seemingly lifting. Natori nodded, turning the sword vertically. She focused on it, imagining the sword levitating in the air as if it were the air itself. When she let go, it wobbled a bit, but stayed regardless. Natori sighed in relief, and then stared at the blade. She blushed, embarrassed that she had to say it in front of such powerful beings, but she closed her eyes anyway.

"To the giver and supplier of all life, I beseech thee, to see me, your humble servant, as worthy enough to wield your heavenly sword so that I may deliver your enemies into your hand... May my blade be as your word, quick and powerful, and sharper than any two edged sword..."

Natori opened her eyes, and the sword began to glow an iridescent white. The blade itself thickened, and a white, translucent ribbon attached itself to the handle. An onyx rose bloomed on the blade directly above the handle. It was beautiful, and pure. So much so, that Natori actually felt bad about wielding such a sword in its current state. But what she did next, would balance it. Purity and corruption, working together within one blade to bring about the end of evil.

Natori liked the thought of that.

If her first mantra formed this, then her second one would mold and contort the sword in such a way that it would change the appearance, but it would work for the

72

same purpose. The weapon was as good or evil as the person wielding it, and Natori knew that she was fighting on the side of good.

"To the ruler of death and destruction, I entreat thee, to bequeath to me your unholy darkness so that I may send my adversaries into the fiery pits of the abyss..."

Pyro and Demetrius were stunned, but that they did not fail to notice the difference in the two mantras. The sword glowed red then, and a black translucent ribbon extended from the handle.

Natori smirked at her proven theory. "This is super sexy. I'm calling it *Rŭze Trn*."

Demetrius looked to Pyro, who watched as Natori grabbed her newly formed blade and flawlessly twirled it. She moved her body along with the movement of the blade, almost as if she were dancing. None of the others had even attempted what she had just performed. Combining the abilities of two enemies to complete a great purpose. She was her father's daughter indeed. Intelligent, and willing to attempt the unthinkable in order to see if a theory would turn into a disaster, or a miracle. Natori, after learning everything she needed to learn, would be a force to be reckoned with. Both Pyro and Demetrius were proud as they watched her twirling her sword gracefully.

Pyro cleared his throat, making Natori turn to him. "Perhaps it is time to escort you to your class. Your first lesson is politics, which is Dawson's domain. Follow us."

Natori nodded obediently and sheathed *Rŭze Trn* within her sheath. It slid back smoothly, and she strapped it around her waist before she followed her leaders out of the infirmary towards her first class. Upon walking out of the infirmary, Natori stopped completely stunned. The halls to the school were completely different to the halls she was used to. The floors were a thick crème carpet for one, and the warm brown walls were lined with pictures of her family. There was one of Pyro and Demetrius standing in front of what looked like a newly built manor. Another picture was one her father, holding a sword. He looked like he hadn't wanted to take the picture, hence his less than excited face. His sword was bluish black, and dark flames spiraled around the blade.

"Kuran Kaji..." Natori smiled, gazing at the teenage version of her father.

Pyro smiled as he followed her line of vision. "Yes, Akiko was a lot like you during his time here. Very hot-tempered, ended up in my office plenty of times for fighting. He always had a valid explanation though so I never really could punish him for it. He was quiet, and usually kept to himself unless he was goofing off with his older brother Blake, or interacting with one of his brothers or the few friends that he had... But that was before he had children. We should hurry, before you are too late."

Natori nodded obediently and ventured further down the hall. They passed two doors, and stopped at the third to their left. Upon opening the door, Natori couldn't help but gaze at her uncle's classroom. The walls were pale blue, and the floors were sandy, with seaweed and coral reefs sitting about. The other students turned to the intrusion, and Natori didn't fail to notice the oxygen bubbles. They were underwater, and the lights in the room acted as the sun, reflecting beautifully off of the ocean floor.

"This... Is way cool!" Natori exclaimed.

"Ah yes," Pyro started. "I had forgotten to mention this... Each classroom is surrounded by the instructor's elemental infinity. Dawson has infinity with water, and as a child he would spend his days surrounded by water. Hence the sun's reflection and the ocean floors... So yes, in Dawson's class, you are literally underwater. But do not worry about breathing, as you can see, no one is having trouble."

Natori analyzed the class once more, and she noticed the fish that swam around, hiding within the seaweed and the coral reefs. It was all so amazing, as Natori herself had

74

often enjoyed the hot summer days when she went swimming with her father and Connor.

Connor.

Natori's eyes took on a sad light as she thought about her first and best friend in the entire world. She wondered if he thought about her, or if he even knew that she was gone. She wondered how his life would be, now that she was no longer a part of it. Would he always remember their friendship? Or would time slowly wipe her from his memory?

Perhaps it was for the best that he didn't remember her. She would be devastated if anything were to happen to Connor, especially if she were the cause to such a tragedy. Perhaps he would graduate, go to college and get drafted like he wanted, find a beautiful wife and have great kids and live happily ever after. She would like that.

Pyro ruffled her head gently. "Alright, we will leave you to your classes now."

"Try not to hit anyone!" Demetrius told her as he followed his older twin back down the hall.

Natori sighed fondly, and she entered the classroom. As her great-grandfather mentioned, she had no trouble breathing even though she was underwater. She didn't have trouble staying on the ground either. Her clothes didn't even feel like they were wet.

"Ah, my darling niece," Dawson greeted, sitting his book down and walking over to her.

"Učitel…" Natori greeted formally with a slight bow of respect.

"Žák, welcome to my domain, we were just about to discuss the alliances of each ethnicity of supernatural beings. I am sure that you know the clichés concerning such things?" Dawson asked.

"Yes, I have heard them." Natori answered.

Dawson's eyes turned sad. "You are uncomfortable in my presence…"

Natori sighed, but nodded truthfully. She didn't want to be uncomfortable, but whenever she was in his presence, her mind immediately went back to her panic attack. It raised her guard and put her on edge.

"I… Keep going back to that time… I hadn't been that scared in very long time…" Natori told him softly, lowering her head.

Dawson pulled her into his embrace, and his arms engulfed her entire upper body. It reminded her of whenever her own father would hug her, and the parental warmth and universal symbol of protection soothe her. She took a deep breath, and hugged him back, noting that her arms would not be able to go fully around his back.

"I apologize. It was not my intention to do so. As I told you, there was an unwanted presence with intentions to harm you, and I had to unleash my aura to redirect it to me so that I could kill it. I am truly sorry for frightening you *láska…*"

Natori felt as if a missing puzzle piece had been placed in its proper place, and that she was one step closer to forming the full picture. When she thought back, she had the same feeling whenever she recovered a cloaked memory. Closing her eyes, she let herself seemingly fall through space and time, until she reached the place where the veil of her memories would momentarily part, revealing to her pieces of her past.

'Natori ran through her home with childish glee. Her biggest uncle had come to play with her while her daddy cooked in the kitchen. They were playing tag, and her uncle was it. She could hear stomping as her uncle tried to catch her, and she was sure that her father could hear them running through halls from the kitchen. Natori ran back down the stairs and into living room, screaming happily when big arms suddenly picked her up. She giggled as her

76

uncle swung her from side to side, his arms engulfing her entire body and keeping her safe and sound.

"Láska! Surely your father believes us to be monsters stomping through his upstairs halls!" Dawson cooed.

Natori laughed. "Daddy says that he'll protect me from the monsters with all of his swords!!!"

Dawson chuckled. "Well if that is the case, then you must stop screaming so loud! Or else your father might come in here and attack me! He may think I am a monster with the intent of eating you!!!"

Natori screamed happily at the prospect of her father attacking her uncle because he thought that he was a monster trying to eat her. The two laughed, looking to the kitchen door where Akiko stood with his arms crossed, looking at them with a blank face. Natori stared back at her father wide eyed, while Dawson held her protectively. Akiko shook his head and smiled softly, and Dawson relaxed his hold slightly.

"I just came in to tell the monsters that lunch was ready, so that they didn't have to find anything to eat, namely my daughter." Akiko informed them.

"Oh good," Dawson told him, looking back at Natori. "Because she would've made a fine meal!"

"Daddy the monster's gonna eat me!!!" Natori exclaimed, reaching towards him with her small hands.

Akiko walked over to them and grabbed Natori from Dawson's arms, shaking his head.

"Idiot." He sighed as he walked into kitchen with a giggling Natori.'

The memory faded, and Natori looked up to her uncle in a new light. She giggled and pulled back, shaking her head at the fond memory.

"I take it that you've recovered a memory, care to tell me what it was?" Dawson asked.

Natori shook her head. "We were monsters."

Dawson laughed and ruffled her hair. "Yes, I remember that as well, now, have a seat. I'm sure you are eager to learn."

Natori nodded and obediently sat in the first empty seat she saw. It was beside another girl that wore the same uniform as she did. Her raven hair was curly and seemed short, but Natori knew better. If she stretched one of the coils, the length of it would have most likely reached the girl's mid back. Her ice green, slit eyes foretold that she was of course nonhuman. Her aura was kind and bashful, with a love of learning and having full knowledge of something before making a decision. She was meticulous, and calculating, as if she had a major purpose that she had to fulfill. Natori smiled as she visibly relaxed next to her, and concluded that being able to detect one's aura so clearly was quite useful. She had always been able to detect something off about a person, which was why during her mundane life she had never really had friends. Natori shrugged indifferently at the way her human life had been, and focused on the lecture her uncle was about to give.

"Now, before you joined us, we were discussing the different allied forces of each ethnicity. This lecture would be good in case any of you find yourselves in a difficult situation; you would know which nonhumans you may comfortably dwell with, and which you would be better off not encountering. For instance, vampires and lycans, or in simpler terms, werewolves. Most believe that these two tribes are natural born rivals. This is not the case, don't let humans fool you; they know absolutely nothing about the political stand points of our kind. Anyway, vampires and lycans are actually allies. They have such a bond, that many marry each other and either lives within the same community, or within close proximity. If an outsider foolishly angers either clan, the other will not hesitate to eliminate them; such is their natural temperamental nature."

Natori had to admit, this lecture didn't make her want to jump out of the nearest window. It was actually fascinating learning about the different alliances that were either established or in the process of being established. It was amazing learning the truth of things one would think imaginary. She felt something brush passed her feet, and she wrinkled her brow and looked down, curious as to what had passed her feet.

Natori screamed in horror, pulling her feet into her seat. "What the hell is that thing!?"

The class erupted into laughter, and Natori blushed, embarrassed. The girl that was next to her smiled kindly, and patted her shoulder sympathetically.

"It's alright; it's just Mr. Dawson's pet blob fish. Don't worry; we've all had the same reaction. It takes some… Getting used to."

"Yeah," Natori sighed, putting her feet back down. "No kidding."

Dawson rolled his eyes as he watched the unique creature glide underneath his desk. "I'll have you know that Betsy is quite comfortable with the way she looks."

Natori shuddered in response, making the girl laugh once more.

"I'm Bryanna, heiress to the eastern lycan tribe. What's your name?" Bryanna asked.

"I'm Natori Hana Sukimori; it's nice to meet you Bryanna." Natori greeted with a smile.

"Another Sukimori? Cool. You're the only girl in the history of your tribe right? I think Mr. Akiko told us something about a prophecy concerning the first female born Sukimori."

Prophecy?

Natori smiled, despite being unnerved at the possibility of her being a part of a prophecy. Instead, she refocused her attention on the rest of her uncle's lecture, absorbing as much as possible. When he was finished, she recounted everything he had said in her notes. Lycans and vampires were allies, and they were allied to the Sukimori tribe. They were beginning to establish an alliance with the mermaids, who would in turn attempt an alliance with the dragons. Sukimori and dragons were great alliances, which resulted in bad blood between Sukimori and mermaids. No one wanted to start a war with Sukimori, since they were one of the first generations of preternatural creatures, and are the guardians of every ethnic group in every realm but one. Wizards and Sukimori were also allies. Sukimori and Takahashi were mortal enemies, but some of the Takahashi wanted an alliance with the Sukimori. The bell rung and Dawson sighed as his students stood to their feet and began to pack their bags.

"Alright, tomorrow we will dive deeper into the Sukimori alliances. Have a good day and try not to anger the more easily agitated Sukimori! Natori, my uncle Jikiya is waiting for you. Would you also tell him that I must speak with him after he escorts you to your father's class?"

Natori nodded, and waved to her uncle as she walked out of the classroom. She wasn't surprised, but still amazed that she sat underwater for an hour and a half, and walked out of the room as dry as she was when she walked in.

"Dawson is quite skilled with his infinity to water. Come, I shall escort you to your father's class." Jikiya told her.

Natori nodded and wordlessly followed Jikiya down the hall. While it was true that she was the only daughter in her clan, she never really thought much of it. Akiko had told her that she was the first girl in their family, and that she would be protected and cherished for the rest of her life. He told her that it was nothing to stress about, and that she would find her purpose when she was older.

But now…

Was she some destined fate changer or something? Ugh. She didn't want to think of herself as anything except for what she was. A girl with abilities she had no idea how to use. But if that ended up being the case, it would make her question her father's reason for even procreating her birth. Was she just around in order to fulfill some prophecy? Her brow knitted together in thought.

"Hey, aren't you that girl from Cassie's party? The one who punched her in the face?"

Natori looked up, seeing Shawn coming towards her. His velvet red hair was still to his shoulders, and his golden eyes threatened to draw her in. His aura still held that thin white light surrounded by black, and Jikiya immediately pulled Natori behind him.

"What do you want Marshall?" Jikiya growled.

Shawn stopped, and held up his hands with a smirk. "Whoa, no need to get protective Kiya; I was just greeting an old friend. We danced together at a party of a mutual friend."

"Unless you want a repeat of last week, I suggest you stop calling me by my nickname. Just because you managed to get away from the Takahashi, doesn't mean I trust you. I'll be damned if you're just trying to get close to my grand-niece just to lure her back to your clan."

"I thought we had moved passed this Jikiya, I am *not* like them." Shawn told him.

"And I thought I told you that I still didn't trust you. Tori, you know him?" Jikiya asked her.

Natori narrowed her eyes. "Unfortunately he is telling a truth. We did dance together at a party. I know *of* him."

Jikiya relaxed his stance, but he didn't move from his spot, and he didn't let Shawn any closer. "Good, I don't want to have to kill him for touching you."

"What's going on?" Akiko asked as he walked out of his classroom. He saw Shawn standing in front of Jikiya and Natori, and his uncle was obviously ready to attack the boy if he got any closer to his daughter. Natori herself was on edge as well, and her narrowed eyes told him that she indeed knew Shawn, but it wasn't on good terms. She didn't trust him, but Akiko said nothing, knowing that one word from him would have Jikiya tearing the boy apart.

"Nothing Kiko," Jikiya answered, his eyes never leaving Shawn. "Almost killed Shawn is all."

"Again? Uncle, you should really seek anger management." Akiko tutted.

Natori could tell that this was a conversation her father and granduncle had often.

"Don't tell me how to live my life." Jikiya hissed.

"Oh!" Natori stated suddenly. "Granduncle, uncle Dawson said that he needed to speak with you."

Jikiya nodded and strolled back down the hall to Dawson's class, knowing that Akiko didn't trust Shawn either, and would not hesitate to kill him if the Takahashi somehow got to Natori.

Akiko looked after Jikiya, and shook his head fondly. "Tori come on in when you're ready. Shawn, I really don't know how you manage to piss my family off on a regular basis and still manage to live, but you should really stop unless you want an early death. Oh, and make any kind of pass at my daughter… And I'll murder you myself."

Shawn shuddered as Akiko walked back into his classroom. "Dude… The men in your family are huge."

Natori shrugged. "There are only four slender built men, but I'd rather fight one of my larger counterparts than one of them in all honesty. Now, why do you address me as if we are friends? If I recall correctly, I wanted to slap you into yester-year for disrespecting my best friend."

Shawn gave her a serious look. "Because it is really important that we become friends… If we want to make it out of this alive."

Natori growled and stepped over to him. "Is that a threat?"

"No, it's a warning."

Shawn strolled passed her and down the hall, and Natori looked after him in suspicion. There was something off about that encounter just now. He almost sounded afraid of the prospect of them not working together. He knew something that she didn't, and it most likely had something to do with the Takahashi. No matter how much she didn't trust him, she definitely needed to find out what he knew.

Chapter 7

"When you're not on edge… You're taking up too much space."

Upon entering the classroom, Natori felt a constant breeze. It wasn't a cold breeze, but it was a prominent occurrence. She smiled softly; it reminded her of her father. Connor had told her all the time that he felt like there was a constant wind around Akiko. And admittedly, she felt safe within the gentle winds of her protector. She walked to the middle seat closest to the instructor's desk and sat down. She was glad that Akiko didn't have infinity with water as well. Knowing him, he would probably have a pet more hideous than Betsy.

Like an Angular fish named Ted.

Natori shuddered at the thought.

The students began pouring in, and a girl strolled over to her. She was beautiful. Long platinum blonde hair and sapphire eyes, she would've given Cassie a run for her money had she gone to Richmond. She sat down beside

Natori and looked her up and down, as if she were gazing at some science experiment.

"Hm. I saw Shawn talking to you so I figured you would be something to look at. *Obviously* I was wrong." She sneered.

"Ugh, who called Rumpelstiltskin? *Please* stop making the poor child endure your face." A boy snapped before Natori could.

Natori covered her mouth and giggled profusely, he reminded her of Connor. He would have totally stuck up for her like this boy had just done.

"Hi, I'm Reeze! Don't worry about Sam the hoe; she gets moody with all the girls prettier than her."

Natori laughed out loud, she could already tell that she and Reeze would make a great pair of friends. Reeze's purple hair overlapped his shoulder, and his ice blue eyes sparkled. He was of slender built, but tall with a fiery attitude. He was gorgeous, but Natori could also tell that she was clearly not his type. Sam scoffed and glared at them both before moving to sit in the middle of the classroom.

Natori leaned back in her chair. "Hm. Is Sam short for something?"

"Samantha. She's a third year, most popular girl in the academy, and her current boy toy is Shawn Marshall, residential hottie. She's a witch, both figuratively and literally. She's also the self-proclaimed prettiest girl in school. But I've seen way prettier around here. You for example, and Bryanna. Have you met her yet? She's the heiress to the eastern lycan tribe."

Natori smiled. "Yeah, we take politics together. She's a nice girl, and she is absolutely gorgeous. So is Samantha, physically beautiful, but her overall personality makes her look like Betsy."

Reeze laughed hysterically. "Mr. Dawson's blob fish!? I told him that thing was... A sight."

"Careful," Akiko admonished as he walked passed them to his desk. "My brother cares a great deal for Betsy, and I personally think she is a sweet little thing."

Reeze scoffed. "Mr. Akiko, you know I have a strict policy for not allowing ugly things to think they're pretty. All the years you've taught me I thought you would have known by now."

Akiko chuckled. "Yes Reeze, I know. I see you've taken a liking to my daughter."

"I figured she was, you two have similar auras... I hope someone told the nurse."

Natori laughed. "I try my best not to lose my temper, but I will admit to having a horrible one. Plus my hands are bisexual."

"So are mine, if you talking crap and you're within distance, anybody can get chopped in the throat." Reeze replied.

A powerful gust of wind blew wildly throughout the room, silencing everyone's individual conversation. The students turned to Akiko, who leaned casually against his desk. He nodded, and the students that were standing took their respectful seats.

"Good. Now, I told you all yesterday that we would begin learning Sukimori culture. Because I've taught you all the culture of your tribes and you want to know mine, I will oblige accordingly."

Akiko's markings appeared, and Natori's eyes widened. They were exactly like hers. She could feel his aura rising until it seemingly filled the room, as if he were omnipresent. Her own markings appeared, and Natori touched her cheek as she felt the familiar burning. She still felt a slight discomfort, but nothing she couldn't handle.

Akiko tapped the black rose on his cheek. "The Onyx rose is the symbol of the Sukimori tribe. It represents many things for us. Power, unity, intelligence, perseverance, humbleness, strength, courage, and perception. There are many within the Sukimori tribe that are blessed with spiritual abilities. Empathy is an ability all royal Sukimori possess."

"Empathy?" Natori asked, listening attentively and writing down the important facts.

Akiko smiled. "Yes Natori. Have you ever felt as if you knew when someone was sad? No matter how good they hid their emotions you still knew? Did your friends ever avoid you when they wanted to keep something hidden? Or did you know when someone lied? Or when the paranormal was near?"

Natori nodded slowly.

Akiko nodded. "You are something called an empath, a living instrument in which energies pass through you. Much like myself, and others of your kin."

"Why is it painful… To awaken?" Natori asked quietly, looking up to her father.

Akiko smiled sadly. "Because… It is one of the first methods of toughening us up. We are warriors, guardians; our tolerance of pain has to be extremely high in order for us to protect all of creation."

"From what?"

"… I pray that you never find out." Akiko told her.

His tone wasn't that of a teacher, but of a father, willing to do anything to keep his child out of harm's way. Natori wanted to cry, but she held it in. Something told her that she would find out, and that there wasn't anything that her father could do to stop it. In fact, she wouldn't be surprised if she already knew.

"Are we many?" Natori asked to change the subject, and the air around them lifted from the tension.

"Yes, there are many of us. But they are not Sukimori, there are only 12 Sukimori, and we are royalty. The others are cousins to our tribe, the Yashimaru. They possess strength, speed, and infinity to one element. They cannot control all elements like Sukimori can."

Akiko demonstrated by holding out his hand. Fire, air, water, earth, and lightning surrounded his palm in one powerful, well controlled circle.

"Do not think that we are able to just control the elements however. Sukimori has infinity to the element they most identify with. In order for us to be able to control other elements we must first subject ourselves to it. So, in my brother Mr. Blake's terminology, Sukimori are thieves and masochists. It takes pain to gain power, and we are able to absorb any form of magic we find useful. I know I always warn you all against this, but *never* anger a Sukimori. We could steal your abilities, weaken you in the process, and kill you. Or we could always just beat you to death. We Sukimori are a generally calm people, but we are also vicious, and we don't back down."

Natori nodded in agreement. "So I don't have a problem with my temper? I'm just naturally vicious when I'm angry?"

Akiko gave her a look. "I'm not saying that, but yes, you are just naturally vicious when you're angry... Now we do have a short fuse, some are shorter than others, such as Jikiya and Dawson. Others are much longer than they should be, namely Sebastian. But all in all compared to the others you and I are in between."

"Is that why you all are gorgeous? Because you can steal magic?" Reeze asked.

Akiko smirked and tossed his hair back. "No, that's just good genetics."

"What's the order of the Sukimori? Like hierarchy." Someone asked.

Akiko crossed his arms and sat down on his desk. "The leader of the Sukimori tribe is Pyro Sukimori, the Head advisor is Demetrius Sukimori. As you all know they are twins. Heir to the throne is Jikiya Sukimori, and his brother, my father, is next in line, Jeremiah Sukimori. Then they are his five sons. Princes Dawson, Blake, myself, Alex, and

Ashten; the younger two are also twins. Then there are my kids, Princes Yukaro and Sebastian, and Princess Natori Sukimori."

Natori growled suddenly. *"Proklínám vás a váse vysokỳ gen."*

Akiko laughed hysterically. *"Tebe taky med!"*

Natori smiled, turning to Reeze who gave her inquiry look. "What is it?"

He simply pointed between her and her father.

Natori giggled. "I said 'curse you and your tall gene.' And he said 'I love you too honey.'"

"Speaking of curses," Samantha suddenly prompted. "What happens if a witch curses a Sukimori?" She asked, glaring pointedly at Natori.

Akiko smiled, but it wasn't friendly. Natori knew all too well what that particular smile meant. She could feel her stomach knotting at the static that charged her father's aura once more. Wind began to whip about angrily. The knot in her stomach tightened in discernment.

"F-father…"

"It is quite alright my daughter. As for your question, Miss Samantha… We would actually turn the curse back to the caster, and more than likely intensify it. We could also destroy the curse completely and end you. Whichever makes us feel better. We could also morph the curse into a flesh-eating disease and send it among your people for even attempting to curse one of us. Or we could do all of them, just to name a few options for you. I know if it were me that stood so assaulted I would morph the curse, and eliminate the caster as well the entire tribe, and my daughter would do the same. Not to mention that such a thing would result in voiding the treaty between Sukimori and namely witches. A war would commence, and we would wipe you all out. So whatever you're thinking of doing… *Don't.*" Akiko warned, letting his eyes narrow dangerously.

The door to his classroom opened, and Jeremiah leaned against the doorframe nonchalantly. Natori knew better however. She knew that her father's temper was horrible, especially whenever she was involved. Sometimes it was so bad that he would have to lock himself in his room until he calmed down. If not…

Someone would end up dead.

Natori raised her hand, remembering an earlier conversation.

"Yes Natori what is your question?" Akiko asked her.

He could tell by her eyes that their conversation would get very ugly if he answered wrong.

"I was in Politics, and a new friend of mine told me about a prophecy concerning the Sukimori princess?"

"Ah yes," Akiko started. "There was a prophecy given to the leader of our tribe. The lone princess of the Sukimori tribe, along with her *parabati*, would bring about the end of war, and peace would forever reign."

"Mhm…" Natori prompted, her eyes beginning to tint red.

Her gaze hardened, and she rested her hands under her chin, much like she did whenever she was about to fight. Akiko knew that stance well, and his eyes widened at the realization of her question.

"No, Tori. I did not facilitate your birth for the sole purpose of a fulfilling a prophecy. I only remembered years later."

Natori sighed through her nose and looked away, and Akiko sighed. She believed him, he knew that, but she was also overwhelmed. All of this was so new to her, and she was trying her hardest to process everything that they had revealed to her. Not all of her memories had been recovered, but the process was too slow for her. He wanted to reassure her.

"You are my daughter, not a simple pawn to be played when the time is right. You know me better than that."

"Do I?" Natori asked, looking up at him. "Because I feel I like I'm just meeting you for the first time."

Akiko smiled sadly. "Don't be the way. I'm the same man you grew up with. The only thing you didn't know was that I have abilities that were passed down to you."

"That's *not* all I didn't know…" Natori sighed as she hung her head.

"We will converse more on the subject later, right now, the bell is about to ring signaling lunch time."

The bell rung and Akiko smiled. "Have a good day class! And behave!"

"Bye Mr. Akiko!" Reeze exclaimed, pulling Natori out of the classroom and towards the cafeteria.

The tension in Akiko's classroom was thick enough to cut through with a knife, and Natori growled irritably. He was keeping something from her, and no matter how well he hid it or denied it, she knew that he was hiding something vital from her. Once they were down the hall, Reeze turned and placed both of his hands on Natori's shoulders.

"Hey, I'm sure that whatever Mr. Akiko is keeping from you is for your own good. Don't sweat it."

Natori wrinkled her brow. "What are you?"

Reeze laughed. "I'm a warlock honey! We specialize in auras! Yours was like a storm cloud of thought, and I could tell that Mr. Akiko was neglecting to mention something. Now come on princess, let's hurry and get our food before the lines get too long."

"Reeze… I'm not really comfortable with the term 'princess' just yet. I'm just Natori, that's all."

"You aren't 'just' anything Natori. Being royalty is a big responsibility, but that is your title. You are the sole princess of the Sukimori tribe. When your subjects come within a few feet of you, they will address you as such." Bryanna told her as she met them in the hall outside of the cafeteria door.

92

"Hi Bryanna," Natori smiled sheepishly. "I'm glad that I at least have two people that remotely like talking to me. I don't feel so alone now."

Bryanna smiled. "Don't worry about it. You've got a kind soul, and if Reeze likes you, then you're automatically one of my friends. Shall we go?"

The cafeteria was unlike anything she had ever seen before. It was outside in a garden surrounded by trees. The air was clean and smelled of rare flowers. The tables were made of logs, with comfortable-looking chairs surrounding them. The lunch station was between two large trees, and the food was scentless until Natori, Reeze, and Bryanna walked over to it. Natori felt them passing through a barrier, and then the delicious aroma of all sorts of food danced around her nostrils. Come to think of it, she hadn't eaten at all since she had woken up, and her stomach growled in protest.

"Wow! Everything smells amazing!" Natori grinned as she took a plate.

Reeze and Bryanna did the same, and then she followed them to a table in one of the corners of the room. It was a table with three chairs, and they took their respective seat.

"So," Bryanna started. "How do you like it so far?"

Natori sighed. "So far I am enjoying myself, which is more than I can say about mundane school. The lectures here are fascinating, and I am enjoying learning about things I never thought I'd truly know about. I am a little peeved that I have to start restart the graduation process, but I believe that it will be well worth it. Especially now with everything going on."

"What's earth realm like?" Bryanna asked.

Natori sighed. "This is a lot better. Less ignorance, much less ignorance. For one thing, there is no pollution here; while on Earth realm it's like an economical wasteland. Earth realm people are so fragile and weak, and they are easily manipulated. However, there are some humans who are none of what I just named. Some humans are kind, and strong, with a strong sense of justice and an unbreakable sense of honor. But those humans are rare. However, there are some things that are similar. I never felt like I truly fit in there, and while I don't particularly fit in here, I have more of a chance to adapt here then I did there. I feel like somehow... I'm home."

"Of course you do," A new voice joined the conversation. "Because you *are* home *Korunní klenot*. This has always been your home, no matter how far my brother spirited you away."

The trio turned to find the youngest son of Jeremiah closing the distance to their table.

Ashten Gokana Sukimori.

"Hi uncle Ashten!" Natori exclaimed, standing up and hugging him tightly.

Ashten engulfed her within his slender arms, looking to see Bryanna and Reeze waving, though Bryanna was more platonic. Natori had suddenly gone deathly still, and he held her to him, knowing that she was recovering yet another memory.

'Akiko opened the door, holding his excited toddler in his arms. He had told her that her uncle Ashten was coming to see her today, and she was bouncing in his arms. Ashten stood on the other side, and Natori's eyes sparkled at the sheer beauty he held.

"Hi my baby!" Ashten exclaimed, taking hold of the young girl and relieving Akiko of the bouncing ball of energy.

"Hi uncle Ashten! Are we going to sing some more today!?" Natori asked.

Ashten smiled. "Of course we are! Now come on let's go into the living room while your papa finishes his work ok?"

"Ok!" Natori giggled.'

Natori pulled back, her eyes beginning to water. "You taught me how to sing…"

Ashten smiled gently. "Yes, I hope that you are still singing."

Natori nodded, beginning to wipe her eyes of the tears that had involuntarily begun to spill.

Ashten hugged her again. "How are you liking school? I see you made some friends."

Natori smiled and pulled back. "Yeah, but I'm sure that Bryanna and Reeze are the only friends I'll have."

Ashten wrinkled his brow. "Why? Big brother says that you are still just the sweetest girl! And Reeze likes you; do you know how hard it is to get Reeze to like anyone?"

"I like you too Ashten!" Reeze exclaimed.

Ashten narrowed his eyes. "No. Your feelings towards me are completely different than your feelings for my niece. And as I've told you before, it is against school rules to date a student, and I'd be robbing the cradle. Ew. Not to say you aren't cute Reeze, but you're too young for me. The person you find will be just for you. Be patient."

Natori nodded her head logically. There were times when she had to explain to young boys that she was too old for them and that when they found their true love, that they would be much better than her.

"Hey." A voice chirped.

Natori felt a jolt, and she turned to see Shawn walking to their table. She could also see Samantha glaring heatedly at her, and then she understood. Samantha had told her that she had seen their earlier encounter in the hallway, and she misunderstood their conversation. The tension rose, and her two new friends were at her side.

"Have you given any thought to my proposal?" Shawn asked her.

Natori shrugged. "I haven't really the time I'm afraid. My schoolwork and your girlfriend got in the way. By the way, I suggest speaking to her before she gets in my face again. I've slammed people through lockers for much less."

"I don't have a girlfriend, why are you volunteering for the position?" Shawn grinned.

"You wish, so Sam isn't your girlfriend? She certainly believes you to be hers."

"Sam's old news, I've encountered someone much more interesting…" Shawn smiled, looking pointedly at Natori.

Reeze stepped in front of Natori and crossed his arms. "And yet you still pant after her like a dying man."

"She's easy, but isn't this the pot calling the kettle black? Considering the amount of panting you do after Ashten it's almost as if he's giving you something that no other student gets."

Natori growled angrily. "Are you implying that my uncle is having sex with a student!?"

Reeze only smiled, and grabbed Natori's hand as she went to punch him. She glared at Reeze, only to pale. Both of them felt the angry aura, and it was as if Natori could hear the crashing waves.

Shawn paled as well, and he turned just as a fist met his jaw powerfully. Natori winced at the sickening 'pop', and the force of it slammed Shawn against the table before he tumbled unceremoniously to the ground.

Ashten crossed his arms. "Sorry, I thought your mouth would protect your face. Bitch."

"Ugh! Ashten I was kidding!" Shawn exclaimed painfully, rubbing his dislocated jaw.

"Malý bratr." Another voice called, joining the conversation.

The group looked over to Ashten's older twin brother Alex as he came to stand by the table beside his brother. The two really were clones of the other. Both administrators wore matching light green shirts with black skinny jeans and light green converse.

Alex giggled. "I have informed Shawn time and time again that my youngest brother is the most likely to hit someone."

Ashten growled. "I've also told plenty of people to not let this pretty face fool them I have the same dad as Dawson."

"I was only kidding though! You dislocated my jaw!" Shawn complained.

The twins gave him a blank look.

"You're lucky I didn't break it." Ashten told him.

Reeze and Bryanna laughed hysterically, and Natori sighed. She helped him to his feet, and then rotated his jaw until it popped back into place.

"Ah! Thanks… How'd you know to do that?" He asked her.

Natori shrugged. "My father is Akiko Yoru Sukimori, do you have any idea have many times I've had to relocate someone's jaw?"

Shawn nodded logically.

"Ah yes," Alex chirped suddenly, turning to Natori. *"Neteř*, grandfather and granduncle requires your presence outside after lunch."

Natori turned to her uncles. "Hm? Why?"

Ashten smirked. "Because sweetie, your training begins."

Chapter 8

"Be careful of your past, it may affect your future…"

Connor was worried.

He hadn't seen Natori since the night he took her home to Akiko after Cassie's party. That had been weeks ago. He'd tried asking around, but it was as if everyone had suddenly forgotten that Natori had ever existed. He sat in class with a defeated sigh, looking at the door every time it opened. Natori had practically prayed for their last day as high school seniors, and now that it had finally arrived… She was gone.

"I want to graduate more than I want to breathe right now."

Connor smiled endearingly at her haste to finish school. He barely paid attention to the lecture of graduation conduct. It was as if Natori had been wiped off of the face of the earth, and he was worried about his dear friend. Besides, he still needed to tell her how he truly felt. He wondered if she had known already, everyone else did. His football buddies picked on him all the time about his feelings for her. But he couldn't really focus on that right now.

Natori had disappeared.

And no one remembered her.

When the bell rung, Connor stood and quickly gathered his things. He figured that he would go to her house, and ask her why she hadn't been coming to school, and why didn't anyone remember her. He had tried her cell, but it said that the number never existed. So, the only logical course of action would be to go to her house and see for himself. Right?

Right.

Connor moved swiftly through the sea of bodies, quickly exiting the building and moving towards his car. He had gotten to the student parking lot when he heard his name.

"Connor!"

He turned to see Cassie running towards him, she was in her cheerleading uniform, obviously on her way to practice. She still wanted to rekindle their relationship, and it was still a no-go for Connor. There was only one girl that was truly for him, and that girl had somehow been wiped from everyone's memory.

Everyone but him.

"What do you want Cassie? I'm busy." Connor asked her, clearly annoyed.

"Are you still chasing after that mystery girl?"

"That *mystery* girl is my best friend Cassie, and I'm not going to stop searching until I find out what happened to her. I know you have a hard time caring about anyone but yourself, but you really should try it sometime, maybe you'd be more likable."

Cassie sighed; she knew that once Connor made up his mind about something there was no stopping him. "Where are you going? So I know what to tell coach when he asks why his star quarterback is missing."

"Tell him I had an emergency, I'm going to her house. It's at the end of the neighborhood." Connor told her as he dug into his pockets for his car keys.

Cassie wrinkled her brow. "Connor… That house burned down two years ago. The family that lived in that house was trapped within the flames."

Connor froze. "… What…?"

"I can't believe you don't remember that! Connor I think you should see a brain doctor." Cassie laughed as she made her way back towards the football stadium.

Connor stayed put. Could Natori have been but a figment of his imagination the whole time?

No.

He had to find out for himself.

Getting into his car, Connor sped out of the school parking lot and down the road. He drove to the neighborhood he knew all too well and drove towards the end. Cassie was wrong! She had to be playing with him!

Cassie was right.

The house where Natori used to live was burned down. Ashes were littering the ground, and he could see the charred remains of support beams. Teddy bears and flowers were among the ruins, the neighborhood paying their respects to the family who had lost their lives. Connor couldn't believe what he saw. He'd been to this very place numerous times, he remembered having dinner with Akiko and Natori, and Akiko making him stay the night when he was too drunk to drive. He remembered how he and Natori would dance in her room when they were smaller, and he remembered when he convinced her to go to her first party.

Was all of that truly his imagination?

All of those precious memories…

Lies?

No…

He refused to believe that. Natori was *not* just some figment of his imagination. She was real, and he would find her.

"Hm. You can't be human if you remember her so profoundly."

Connor whipped around, how did they get behind him without his hearing them!? A fist blackened Connor's world, and he fell to the unforgiving concrete with a thud.

"They must have been close…" The voice from earlier told his companion.

"Hmmm… He'll be nice bait. Natori would never allow harm to come to this one. He'd definitely be enough to draw the little bitch out from under Pyro's protection." The companion replied.

"Indeed. Shall we depart?"

"Yeah, I'm sick of smelling the disgusting scent of humans."

The doors opened, and Natori strolled out of the manor with Ashten and Alex behind her. Lunch had ended, which meant that classes resumed for other students. Natori however, would be training with the leaders of their tribe. The older twins were standing side by side in the middle of an open field. The earth looked a little worn, which meant that it was the designated training area for all students.

"Good afternoon *vůdce, hlava poradce.*" Natori greeted.

They made a face.

"Ew. Don't ever address us so formally again. We're your great grandfather and uncle. Only subjects address us so formally." Pyro told her.

"Oh, I'm sorry… Hi great grandfather, hi great granduncle. Is that better?" Natori asked.

Pyro and Demetrius smiled broadly. "Hi Tori! Hi little twins!"

"Hi big twins! We brought little Tori!" Alex and Ashten smiled.

"Good. Now please go back inside and check to make sure that the protection spells are holding up."

Ashten and Alex nodded and headed back to the manor, leaving Natori alone with the older twins. Pyro wore a white muscle shirt with red basketball shorts, and his hair was tied into a ponytail. Demetrius wore a dark green muscle shirt and white basketball shorts. His red hair was also in a ponytail, and both he and Pyro wore the same shoes. Natori could see where her father had obtained his obsession with basketball shorts from. He had over thirty pairs of them in his closet.

"Alright, today is the today that you officially begin your training. Demetrius and I will be your instructors and we will make sure that you become fully capable of controlling the abilities passed down from your father. The abilities you gained from your mother however, will have to be sharpened elsewhere, and we will send you to that particular place after your training here is complete. Are you retaining everything so far?" Pyro asked.

Natori nodded, listening attentively to everything her leader explained to her. Demetrius handed her a set of clothes, and she went behind the tree to change. When she emerged, she was wearing a simple red tank top and spandex. It was comfortable, and Pyro wrinkled his brow.

"Yeah I know." Demetrius sighed, shaking his head.

Natori looked down at herself. "What is it?"

"Nothing dear, we're just old as hell. Anyway, before we really get started, there are some things that we must do. Firstly, we must find your element's infinity, which will be easy. Just do exactly as I tell you and you'll be fine ok?" Demetrius instructed.

"Yeah, I got it." Natori told them.

"Ok, so what I want you to do is close your eyes, and think about the each individual element. You'll feel a connection to one, then it'll begin to manifest. Simple."

Natori nodded and closed her eyes. Clearing her mind, she began to think about each element individually. Water was her first thought. She thought about how the beautiful, yet powerful waves crashed against the rocks of the shore, and how the deep blue sea kept extraordinary things hidden. Such as creatures thought to be extinct, wreckage, and priceless jewelry. She thought about how it felt to be surrounded by miles and miles of water, flowing leisurely through the watery abyss. It reminded her of her brother Yukaro, he was beautiful, and held deep, mysterious emotions. As if he were somehow lost at sea, a sea of his own mental distress. It reminded her of her uncle Dawson, and how he so effortlessly did everything. Water was just that, effortless.

Flawless, like her twin uncles.

And her brother Sebastian, but for him, it was a darker tone.

But she *felt* nothing.

No profound connection to it.

The next element that graced her thoughts was wind. It reminded her so much of her father, and she remembered the days that they danced together outside, the wind deciding their movements and how she tried to be as graceful as her father was. If Akiko was nothing else, he was a brilliant dancer. It never ceased to amaze her that such a burly man could hold such grace and elegance. Connor would often tell her that her father was a contradiction. He was so powerful, and yet so graceful that it was alarming. She marveled at how the wind could be so graceful, but hold so much destructive power. She noticed how the wind whipped about angrily around her father whenever he became irritated. She had gotten the same aura around her great granduncle.

Again, she felt nothing.

104

Earth was her next place. She loved how the sand felt beneath her feet, and the way the grass tickled her when she and Connor used to go cloud gazing. The earth was stagnant, stubborn and unmoving, much like her uncle Blake could be at times. She suddenly remembered some of the conversations he and her father had whenever he would come over. She thought about the mountains, and how they stood tall and unmoving, much like her great grandfather. Still yet, nothing.

The last element was fire. It was Natori's favorite element. She loved how the oranges, yellows, reds, and golds mixed together to create blazing heat. She loved how fire sustained all forms of life, that without fire, humanity would be completely lost. She marveled at how fire could be thought about in different forms. The truth for example, the truth sometimes hurt, most times it burned. It consumed everything around it, and it was the purest form of cleansing. She imagined herself surrounded by flames, letting the heat warm her skin so completely. She felt as if she were inside of a warm cocoon, a simple caterpillar waiting to become a butterfly. She thought about the destructive ability of fire, and how if one was not careful, it could reduce an entire plain to ash. Much like…
Her.

Connor had always told others to be careful of her temper, and that it was as if she burst into flames, ready to consume everything around her. She had always been told that she was fiery, and she often described herself as being a fiery person. She was passionate about everything she set her mind to, and lashed out at anyone who disrespected her.

Finally, she felt it. She felt as if something were spiraling around her, engulfing her body in a fiery pillar of protection. She was happy, and she felt her body began to ascend.

"Natori, open your eyes." Pyro told her.

Natori did as commanded, and indeed, there was a fiery pillar spiraling around her, and she had risen a bit off the ground.

"Infinity with fire… As expected of Akiko's daughter." Demetrius smiled.

"Good. Now that we know, fire will be the first ability we sharpen… But there is something that you should know, something I know that Akiko has neglected to tell you, and it will explain a lot of things concerning you and Akiko, all of us." Pyro told her seriously.

Natori nodded, and the flames dissipated. She dropped to the ground, and she waited for Pyro to impart some gem of wisdom. Pyro and Demetrius sat on the ground in front of her, and she of course followed suit.

"As you know," Pyro began. "We are the most powerful beings on the planet. We have to be, being guardians and descendants from Michael."

Natori wrinkled her brow, and then her eyes widened. A grin split her face. "Michael… As in Michael the *archangel*!? Like, his blood runs through our veins?"

Pyro smiled. "No, he is the angel that trained my brother and I, and we passed his teachings on to you all. You know of him?"

Demetrius chuckled; he could see how awestruck she was.

"He's my *favorite* archangel *ever*! Have you met him? What's he like?"

"He's pretty cool. Very serious about following orders and will reprimand us if he sees us falling out of line." Pyro told her.

"I'm sure he'd be a lot nicer to the girl in our tribe though. He's nice to us, but he expects the best." Demetrius added.

Natori nodded. "I hope I live up to his expectations…"

Pyro smiled. "I'm sure you will, now to the topic at hand… You see, in an attempt to stop God from creating us

Lucifer put a curse on us… When we awaken, our powers… Begin to eat at our sanity…"

Natori frowned. "What…?"

Pyro sighed. "This is why Akiko did not want to be the one to tell you… But you had to know. It's happening to you, as it happened with all of us."

"What do you mean it's happening to me? I don't feel insane at all… But father, I've never seen him act out of the ordinary."

Pyro snorted. "Tori he's your father, and you're a girl. You may be tough, but there are some things even you can't handle. Think back, deep down, you've always known something was wrong, maybe he did something or said something or had a certain look in his eyes that would disappear as soon as you tried to focus on it or he'd lock himself in his room for long periods of time or…" Pyro stopped talking, he could tell by how still Natori had become that something he said had triggered a memory.

Natori remembered it clearly. The times Akiko would lock himself in his room, the times she would think he had a crazed look in his eyes, but she had always thought that she was just seeing things because it was gone the moment she tried to focus on it. He would sometimes say things that made her worry, but he had always laughed it off and apologized for creeping her out.

'I love blood. The look of it, the smell of it. It's such a beautiful ruby that I hard time not wanting to see it…'

'Papa…?'

'Hm? Oh sorry! Forget I just said that. Ok?'

There were times when she was younger, that Akiko would come home in the dead of night, soaked from head to toe in a thick red substance. He would enter their home laughing quietly, as if he were remembering a joke someone had told him. Her innocent mind wrote it off all the time.

But now…

107

Natori looked to her companions in horror. "Dad's a... Sociopath..."

Pyro nodded gravelly. "A very violent, serious illness that triggers when he is angered. We've warned the other students about angering him. We've taught our students about our afflictions and the signs to look for. They know the triggers."

"The symptoms began as a child, but that only gives the parent a clue to what kind of illness their child will develop once they awaken," Demetrius started. "For instance, I was diagnosed with antisocial personality disorder... Poor brother... I frequently disobeyed my brother, and played a major role in his mental illness. Come to think of it," Demetrius laughed. "I've probably killed more people than Ted Bundy! But that was the beauty of being a child... No one believes children are capable of such things. I even killed our parents... I still do not know why Pyro helped me get away with it."

Natori covered her mouth. "You... Murdered your *parents*!? Why!?"

Demetrius shrugged. "They were abusive and neglected us frequently, and I got sick of it."

Natori lowered her hand. "... How'd you do it?"

Demetrius smirked. "I poisoned my mother so that she would drown in her own vomit, and I just flat out stabbed my father to death. I don't know why I so merciful towards her..."

Pyro shrugged. "Beats me, she deserved it the most... But over the years we've forgiven them and repented... God understands that Lucifer cursed us, and he knows that we try to live right even with these curses, so he doesn't blame us. It started out as a curse, but it has rooted itself so deep within us that it has become a trait within our family."

"How can you both talk about this so freely? As if we aren't dangers to those around us!" Natori exclaimed.

Pyro wrinkled his brow. "Why not talk freely about it? It is a part of our culture. I'm a sadist. I enjoy torturing men with red hair or emerald eyes, or both. I also enjoy mutilating women with white hair, amethyst eyes, or both."

Natori's blood ran cold. "W… Why?"

Pyro shrugged. "They look just like our mother. Demetrius may be merciful towards women who look like that, but I'm not," he smiled evilly. "What's wrong? Are you worried that I may be tempted to carve your pretty little face like a jack-o-lantern?"

Natori shuddered at the mental images that attacked her mind.

Pyro smiled. "Don't worry honey; I would never harm my own flesh and blood. You may look like someone I hate, but so do I, and I wouldn't harm you anymore than I'd harm myself, because while you do look like her, you do not act like her, and that's one of the things that keeps you safe. That, and I love you deeply, you're my great grand-daughter. I would never hurt you. It takes more than just looks to make me want to kill someone. I have to see characteristics too. Now, we've wasted enough time talking. It is time to begin your lessons."

Natori nodded obediently, standing to her feet. Now that she had awakened, she wondered what kind of mental illness she would have to face. She did have problems forming relationships, mainly with females. In fact, Bryanna was her first female friend. Maybe she would have APD like her great grand-uncle. But she found herself wanting to kill every brunette haired or emerald eyed female that crossed her path because they reminded her of Cassie. Maybe she would be a sadist like her great grandfather. However, she also had developed a love for seeing blood; it was why she watched so many horror films. Maybe she was a sociopath like her father.

Wait…

"What about Shawn?" Natori asked as she followed her leaders further onto the open field.

Pyro chuckled. "Marshall... I tell him all the time that the only reason he hasn't yet become one of my *prized possessions* is because of his allegiance... But that could all too easily fly out of the window the very second I catch him trying to lure you anywhere near the Takahashi, so stay away from him... On second thought, befriend him... I've been wanting to gut him ever since he stepped foot into my manor."

Classes had ended by the time Natori was finished with her lesson. She sighed dejectedly as the previous conversation had stunted her learning process. All she had learned to do was summon her infinity and pour it into her sword.

Pyro smiled as he threw an arm over her shoulder. "Don't worry love! You'll get the hang of it! This is just the first day it takes time and practice in order to truly master such techniques. You're learning quickly!"

Natori sighed and then nodded. "Perhaps..."

But she knew that she needed to become stronger, mentally as well as physically. She needed strength in order to be able to coexist with the illness that would eventually make its presence known. She had just awoken, so she wondered how long it would take until her illness began to manifest.

"So... I awakened to more than just my abilities..." Natori commented.

"Yes, but the awakening process is the most excruciatingly painful process that a Sukimori will ever have to go through. It boosts your pain tolerance to near impossible levels, depending on your mother's species and if you even survive."

"I thought that Sukimori were purebred no matter who the mother was."

110

"That is true," Pyro told her. "However, each Sukimori still receives a trait or two from their matriarch. For example, my sons' mother was a shape shifter, so Jikiya and Jeremiah can change their appearances at will. Your father's mother was a soul shredder, so he and your uncles can see the emotional scars on a person's soul and exploit them at will. Yukaro's mother was a vampire so he has fangs. Sebastian's mother was an angel so he has this purity about him that no one else in the family has. I actually wouldn't be surprised if he didn't have any mental illness like his counterparts... I told Akiko that it was technically incest, but he didn't care. Your mother was-

"A neglectful skank that wanted no part in the life of the child she bore for nine months." Natori spat.

Pyro smirked. "False. Your parents actually made that up so that you'd stop asking about her. Your mother is in fact a high priestess... Chikara is her name."

Natori's eyes narrowed in recognition of the name. "That can't be true... Chikara was the most powerful priestess in the world. She could purify the most powerful of demons as if it were child's play. It was said that her abilities were so powerful that she could purify humans with evil in them. She was so hunted that she had to go into hiding. If Chikara had a daughter she would have been killed by Chikara's enemies, and if dad was their father no doubt the child would grow more powerful than the mother. I have only just awoken and I don't even have a *millimeter* of the power Chikara has, so how could I be the love child of Chikara and Akiko?"

Pyro smirked, leaning against a nearby tree. "Do you recall the dream you had when you first arrived here?"

"Yes... The dream about the snake woman disguising herself as my mother..."

"And her disguise..." Pyro pressed on. "Was it an older version of you with orange hair and gold eyes?"

Natori sliced her eyes towards him. "Yes… How did you know?"

"Because Demetrius and I have met Chikara and that is exactly what she looks like. Akiko never told you her name so the Takahashi thought that they could feed you lies… But they knew that if you at least knew what Chikara looked like, and if you had a subconscious pull to her, then it would confirm their growing suspicion around you. Now go back to the manor, you session is over for today." Pyro told her, turning to Demetrius.

Natori was floored by the new information, and she made a beeline for the manor. She needed answers, and she needed them now.

Chapter 9

"Once the veil is parted, it can never be drawn together again..."

The last bell of the day had rung, and the students were left to their own devices. Akiko was sitting at his desk, grading the latest essay when the door to his classroom was almost torn off of its hinges. He looked up to see Natori stalking towards him, and she was clearly angry. Akiko lowered the essay and wrinkled his brow.

"Natori? Did something happen?" he asked her worriedly.

Natori held up her hands in an attempt to calm herself. There was so much that she had yet to learn and it seemed as if every time she obtained an answer it only deepened the mystery. She could feel herself becoming more and more overwhelmed, and the feeling was so intense that it almost had enough power to bring her to her knees.

Natori took a slow, deep breath. "Father… Why have you kept my mother's identity from me?"

Akiko growled irritably and then sighed. He hadn't wanted to believe Pyro when he had informed him of the Takahashi demons finding a way to contact Natori, but her barging into his classroom confirmed it.

They found her.

"Tori… I…" Akiko sighed, and then tugged at his hair with a furious growl.

Natori knew her father's tendencies all too well. He was having a hard time telling her. He was at war within himself. He wanted to tell her, but something was preventing him from doing so. Some traumatic memory of something happening to someone who *did* know. He knew that she was overwhelmed, and that withholding information could possibly put her at greater risk, but full disclosure would put her at greater risk than only partial disclosure.

She remembered Yukaro. There was something eating at her elder brother, something that their father failed at preventing. She watched Akiko cover his face.

"Yukaro…" Natori whispered quietly.

Akiko glared at her through his hands. *"What about your brother?"* he asked, his voice clipped.
Natori sensed the static once again, and she began to back away from him.

'Your father is a sociopath… Do not anger him…' The voice within her chided.

"It's because of what happened to him… That you refuse to tell me everything… Was it also because of his mom?"

Akiko laughed humorlessly. "No, that was my fault, and I live with what my actions caused him every time I look at him. You see, *moje dcera*, you are a part of a legendary tribe, strike one. *Your* mother and our tribe are the most hated beings within the Takahashi realm, strike

114

two. You yourself are the manifestation of an ancient prophecy given to our leader, strike three." He explained coldly, putting up three fingers. "You were born with three strikes against you, that is why you are so fiercely protected and my reason for withholding certain things from you. It is also why you are taught so brutally… Because while what befell Yukaro was bad… What shall befall you should we ever, for whatever reason let you fall into the wrong hands, will be worse. If the Takahashi can kill you or your *parabati* before you two manage to find each other, then the prophecy will be null and void, and Armageddon would be initiated."

Natori swallowed the lump in her throat and sat down. She took multiple deep breaths, and ran her hand through her hair. "Ok so let me get this straight, if the Takahashi kill me… It'll start the *end of the world!?*"

"Yes, and believe me, they wouldn't be quick about it."

"Oh my God… Why can't I be normal?" Natori asked.

Akiko snorted. "Because normality is boring."

Natori smiled weakly. "Yeah, you're right… But I'd rather be a mermaid or something."

Akiko shrugged. "I'm sorry, but this is the life you have been dealt. No one but you can do this Natori, because if there was, then they would be in your place. You and your *parabati* are the other halves of each other. They need you, and you need them."

"How do I know when I've found them?"

Akiko smiled. "You'll know. Now come, I shall show you were you are to rest."

Natori followed her father out of his class and down the hall. There was so much information that she needed to absorb, not to mention that she needed to find her *parabati* before one of them was killed by the Takahashi and initiate Armageddon. Ugh, it all sounded so far-fetched, but she also knew that Akiko would never lie to her, especially about something like this. Natori knew that she needed to train and learn now more than ever, because if she didn't, it would spell the end of the world. They had just gotten to the staircase of the manor that would lead to the student rooms when a voice stopped their stride. They turned to see Reeze, Bryanna, and Yukaro making their way toward them.

"Hey dad, hey Tori. What're you two doing?" Yukaro asked as they closed the distance.

He seemed perfectly fine, but Natori knew better. There was an underlining depression within him, as if something tormented him on a daily basis. It felt as if so much as waking up was a challenge, and he had to fight every day to keep the memory of what happened to him from devouring him. It was his illness, chronic depression, and it sometimes caused him to lash out violently. Natori looked to their father, and he shook his head discreetly, telling her to 'say nothing about what she felt.' It was obvious that Akiko felt it too, but since he had better insight to the situation, Natori decided that it was indeed better not to say anything.

Akiko shrugged. "Your sister and I were heading upstairs to her room."

Yukaro smiled, but it didn't touch his eyes. "I'll show her father. Besides, I've been meaning to speak with her about something. I won't let her out of my sight. Promise."

Akiko discreetly flinched, and then turned when his name was called. Not only did he see his own father, he saw his entire family save his own children. He knew something was up by the seriousness of their collective aura.

"Hm… Natori, I leave you in the hands of your brother. If either of you need us, we will be in your great-grandfather's office."

Natori nodded and watched as Akiko strolled over to the rest of their family. She waited until they all had disappeared down the hall to turn to Yukaro. His sapphire

116

hair was in a thick ponytail, and he wore a dark blue T-shirt and black skinny jeans with blue converse. He was truly gorgeous, and he appeared radiant as he took her hand.

"Reeze and Bryanna wanted to show you around the manor entirely, but this talk needs to be private. Ok?" Yukaro smiled.

It was not a suggestion, but an order. Natori obediently nodded her head, and waved to her friends before following Yukaro from the staircase and out of the manor. They traveled to the back of the manor where there was a large garden. There were flowers everywhere, and a grassy path in which students were able to walk through without crushing any of the flowers. Yukaro led Natori to a bench where they sat, and he watched his sister admire the vibrant colors of reds, blues, and black flowers that blended with green grass and the medium sized koi pond.

"This is beautiful… To be surrounded by all of this… Creation."

Yukaro smiled. "Isn't it beautiful? Sebastian and I planted this all ourselves. I come here often to think, and to relax. I wanted to talk to you in some place tranquil, I can feel that you have become overwhelmed and stressed."

Natori sighed, and lowered her head in shame. She knew that she was being difficult, and she wished that she was more accommodating. But every answer led further into the mystery, and it was getting harder and harder to constantly adapt to a life she held very little understanding of. Her father, as well as the rest of her family, kept secrets that held the potential to help her navigate through this new life that she was constantly taking blows from.

Yukaro lifted her chin, and wiped away the frustrated tears. "Hey now, don't beat yourself up about how you feel. It does no good, trust me, I've been there. If you ever need to talk, I'm here. Alright? Don't hesitate to come get me."

Natori glanced at him, and then sighed. "… Father says that I was born with three strikes against me. He says that if he, or any of you slips your collective grasp on me that what shall befall me will be worse than what befell you... That the death of me or my *parabati* would be the beginning of Armageddon... But the trouble is... I do not know what befell you... I don't know anything..."

Yukaro nodded with a sad smile. "For you, it would be far worse. Which is why you must trust our father. This isn't easy for him either, and as you now know, he wars with himself about those secrets... I pray that you never find out what happened to me... And I pray that you never experience it."

Natori watched as Yukaro's eyes welled with tears, and she embraced him tightly. She knew what it was like to have to hold something in. To hold such a profound emotion within herself that she would sometimes feel as if she would explode. There was a pooling within her stomach, but she couldn't properly discern the cause of the amount of dread she felt polluting her stomach. Natori pulled back after a bit, and rubbed at her knotting stomach, trying to soothe the pain of discernment.

"Hey... Can I ask you something?" She asked.

Yukaro reached out to rub the back of her neck, and nodded. He could feel that something was bothering her.

"I know about being able to feel the emotional and mental pain of your loved one... But what about physical? Could we feel that as well?"

Yukaro nodded. "Yes, you are able to feel what they are doing to your loved one, and if you close your eyes during that time, you can see who that loved one is."

Connor grunted as his back hit the cold cement of the dungeon. His entire body was practically one giant nerve of pain. He slowly, painfully turned onto his stomach, and then stood to his feet. Connor had regained his vision some time ago, but not within the time it would have took him to determine where they had taken him. Instead, he focused on his surroundings to see if he would be able to guess his location. There were dim lights hanging above him, enough so that he could see, but not clearly. The bars to his cell were oak, and the floor his back had smacked onto was indeed cement.

"You can't be human if you remember her so profoundly."

Had they been talking about Natori?

Were these the creeps following her?

Connor turned to his right at the sound of whispering, and noticed two people conversing on the other side of his cell. They were staring at him with a concentrated hatred, as if they knew something was off about him. One man, who was taller than the other, had black hair and white eyes, as if he were blind but somehow Connor knew better. His skin was pale, and lined with muscle, and he wore a black undershirt and black leather pants with a skull belt. The other had thick red hair that touched his shoulders, and golden eyes that held way too much arrogance. He was darker than his counterpart, wearing a white undershirt with a red leather vest over it. He wasn't as muscled as the pale one, and Connor knew that he would win in a death match between them.

Wait…

"You're that guy from Cassie's party…" Connor said.

'I can't ignore his aura anymore.' He remembered Natori telling him that. Connor slammed his hands against the bars with enough force to make the oak screech in protest. He could break the bars altogether, but he didn't know what would happen to Natori if he did that.

"You're the ones that's been following her! Where is she!? I swear if one hair on her head has been touched I'll—"

Shawn laughed. "I told you he was heels over head for her Zulo, and he's her best friend. Which is why he is perfect."

Zulo, the black haired man, nodded. "Indeed. She's beyond our reach at the moment, but you will change that…"

"I'll never lead you to her!" Connor hissed. He had never really felt as if he had truly belonged, and the only person who he could be himself around was Natori. She was his best friend, and the unrequited love of his life, and he would sooner die than betray her.

Shawn smirked, and nodded to Zulo. Zulo strolled over to Connor's cell and produced a key. He unlocked the cage and caught Connor's fist. "You're just a sniveling human boy, no match for me." He twisted Connor's arm behind his back and grabbed his hair, then threw him to ground beyond the prison. Connor hissed in pain and looked up from the pair of boots in front of him.

Though he didn't show it, he immediately regretted that decision.

Shawn was standing over him with a cruel smile, and in his hand was a knife. Zulo grabbed Connor, struggling to hold him still. Shawn quickly squatted and sliced Connor across his chest, and Zulo released him. Connor fell to the floor and hissed at the feel of cold steel slicing his chest. He panted with both pain and rage, but mostly rage.

"I'm going to slit your throat with that same blade…" Connor growled.

A fiery pain made Connor bellow in agony as it traveled through his body. Tears spilled from his eyes in the intensity of it. With an enraged roar, Connor scrambled to his feet and attacked Shawn. They fell to the floor fighting, and the door to cellar opened. Four more men poured into the room and pulled Connor off of Shawn. He began to convulse, and they lifted him onto a cold operating table. Each of his limbs were strapped down, and Connor wheezed out. Shawn picked himself up off of the floor, and wiped his bleeding mouth. He waited until Connor had stopped convulsing to speak.

"We don't need you to tell us where she is. We already know, we just need you as bait to draw her here. It'll be easy, she'll feel you being harmed and come running to save her *precious* Connor... And you're going to regret damaging my face you sniveling toad."

Connor's heart dropped to his feet. He watched as Shawn grabbed a jagged, but sharp-looking knife and examined it. His heart began beating fast. He remembered the last conversation he and Natori had about pain. He was sitting in class with a stomach virus, and both he and Natori felt it.

Are you alright Con?

Yeah Tori I'm fine.

Connor, you know that I can sense your pain. Come on, tell me what's wrong?

He prayed that she wouldn't feel this.

Chapter 10

"The light is often surrounded by darkness…"

Natori stared up at the ceiling of her room with bored eyes. Three days had passed since her conversation with Yukaro, and the dread in her stomach had not left. In fact, it had become so profound that she was confided to her room for the day. Her family would visit her at different intervals to check on her, and it helped alleviate her boredom until they left.

The room she was in was an exact replica of her old room in earth realm. The sea green walls with her out of place deep purple king-sized canopy bed. The black drawers were there, and her iPod sat on the nightstand next to her bed. Natori had almost wanted to call Connor in her nostalgia, but she knew Akiko wouldn't let her. No matter how thorough her explanation was, she knew that he would never recall their friendship. Her father's abilities were immense.

"I wonder what he's doing right now…"

Connor sputtered as ice cold water was thrown in his face. It had been three days since this hell began, and he had done a good job at keeping his emotions at bay. His wounds were healing from the last session, which baffled him, but it also helped keep his mental and physical distress from reaching either Natori or Akiko.

You're like a son to me boy, if anything happens to you, I'm barging in guns blazing.

"You don't get to faint." Zulo growled, brandishing yet another blade. "But I'll tell you this... You're strong for a human. Most in your situation would be begging for their lives, but not you... But then, you're not human are you? No not at all. I'm thinking you're a werewolf, but we have no way to tell from an embryo. You're keeping your emotions and pain bottled up too, you've must have been friends with Natori for a long time for you to learn how to keep yourself from her."

Connor laughed. "It pays to fall in love with someone you can barely hide things from... You have to learn, mostly for whenever I'm angry with her, but it also comes in handy for this situation Y'know? Because I told you... I will *not* lead you to her... Not willingly."

"Oh that's all fine and dandy but trust me, I'm the best torturer in my clan, and you'll draw her out... That, I promise." Zulo smirked maliciously, examining the knife.

Connor steeled himself, and prepared for the pain.

Ashten walked into Pyro's office holding student files, his face grave. The others were sitting around discussing the latest Takahashi kill.

"Here are the files you wanted grandfather."

124

"Thank you Ashten, now please go stand beside your brother." Pyro told him, looking to Demetrius, who leaned beside him against his desk.

Ashten immediately obliged, and looked to Alex worriedly.

"I don't understand it." Blake sighed, running his hand through his hair. "The Takahashi should not be able to step into our realm."

"But Shawn is able to withstand the purity we naturally give off. In fact, he seems drawn to it in some way." Sebastian interjected.

"We allow Shawn to remain here because he sided with us. Lucky him, I find myself wanting to mutilate him more and more with each passing day." Pyro sighed wistfully. "There is no other reason for his continued existence… No, something is polluting the air…"

"And allowing them to breach our domain." Demetrius finished.

Akiko rubbed at his stomach. The same dread Natori felt had been pooling in his stomach as well. But unlike his daughter, he knew the feeling, and could go for much longer periods of time while afflicted with the emotions of another. But it was still very uncomfortable, and he growled as the feeling grew worse and worse.

"Mŭj syn, what's wrong?" Jeremiah asked.

"Dread… Someone is being harmed… I just—" Akiko suddenly gasped out in a pain so intense that it bought him to his knees. It was as if he were being carved into by some invisible blade.

Jeremiah sunk to his knees beside Akiko. "Akiko! Close your eyes! Who is it? Who's being tortured!?"

"It's—"

"Connor…" A small, pain filled voice called.

The men in the office turned to see Natori leaning against the doorway, one hand clutched her stomach while the other held her weight against the doorframe. Tears spilled from her eyes like a river, and she was panting as if she had either ran a marathon, or was in extreme pain.

Pyro approached her and lifted her into his arms, he then carried her over to a vacant chair and sat her down.

"Who's Connor?"

"Natori's best friend. He's also happens to be like a son to me…" Akiko sighed.

"What have I told you about human ties!? They're dangerous! Now how did he remember you two? Because you told me that every human in earth realm who ever had any contact with either you or Tori would not remember."

"And they don't! No human," Akiko paused for a long time. "I didn't anticipate this." He mumbled suddenly.

"Didn't anticipate what?" Jeremiah asked, helping him to his feet.

"Connor isn't human. He can't be human if he remembers Natori so profoundly, and no doubt he was searching for her… And they found him."

Natori covered her face in devastation. Connor did remember her, and now she was the reason why he was being tortured. She knew Connor, knew how deep his loyalty for her ran. He knew how to hide from her, and held out for three days until he could no longer withstand the pain. It was why the pain she had felt was like a blast through her entire body.

"They're trying to lure Natori to their realm using Connor."

"We have to help him! Father please he's my best friend! We have to save him!" Natori pleaded.

Pyro kneed in front of Natori and placed his hands on her shoulders. "We will liberate your friend Tori, but we have to prepare. Takahashi have been spotted throughout the forest, possibly waiting for you to come running out of the manor so that they can kidnap you. We need to focus entirely on your training now. No more class until you are fully trained."

126

"But Connor—"

"No buts Tori. I know you're worried about Connor, and we will start working on his liberation immediately. But we cannot afford to have you unfocused. That's exactly what they're counting on. If they kill you, Armageddon will start. I need you to bear with me. Ok?"

Natori took a few deep breaths to calm herself before she nodded. She stood to her feet and began to walk out of the room.

"Tori where are you going?" Akiko asked as she reached for the doorknob.

"To get answers."

Later on that day found Alex and Ashten perched up a tree. Their hair was up and out of the way, and they were observing the movements of their current prey. Two members of the Takahashi clan had broken away from the rest of their pack, most likely scouting the area.

"Two intruders to the left side of the forest… Most likely patrolling our lands." Alex whispered.

"Trying to find the best spots to keep under radar… And the best method of speeding up the process of luring our crown jewel from the divine protection." Ashten replied.

"Bastards… They were in her mind once, I bet they'll try to make contact again."

The twins leapt from the branch they were crouched on, and landed in front of the startled Takahashi.

"Are you two lost?" Alex asked.

"I think you bastards missed a turn or two." Ashten jeered.

The Takahashi demons growled, and prepared for a brawl. Alex rushed forward and jabbed one twice then kicked him back into a tree. Ashten tackled the other before he could move to defend his partner. He throttled his hands around the demon's neck and squeezed. Alex kneed his opponent before quickly brandishing a dagger and slicing it across his throat. Blood splattered on Alex's face as the demon slid slowly to the ground. Ashten watched as the demon he was strangling's eyes filled with blood. Strangulation was a slow process, but Ashten adored the sight.

"Poor thing... Should have thought about the dangers of encountering a trained Sukimori."

The dying demon laughed. "You think... This will... Make a difference...? You are only... Prolonging the inevitable... She will... Be ours... And she will die..."

Ashten dug his nails into the demon's neck with a growl. Smirking at the pained groan, he ripped off the skin on his neck, and then stood as the demon bled to death.

"Perhaps they should serve as the last things the Takahashi demons shall see for breaching our lands?" Ashten suggested.

Alex smirked maliciously.

Shawn sat in his room within the fortified manor of the Sukimori tribe, polishing one of his daggers. Connor was strong, and his torture hadn't really gone as planned. He'd thought the toad would be begging for his life by now, but he wasn't. Not only that, but he was hiding his emotions so that Natori couldn't feel him. His wounds were also healing entirely too fast for him to be human. But no one could discern the true origins of an embryo, much like Natori when she was yet still slumbering, Connor was undetectable. Not even Connor himself knew what he was. Shawn was betting on Lycanthrope.

They were known for their regenerative abilities.

There was a knock on the door. He watched as it opened to reveal Samantha. Beautiful and graceful, she moved into his room with poise fit for a goddess, and an arrogance that matched his own. Many of their peers thought that they were made for each other, and Shawn could understand why they would think that. But as of now, his focus was elsewhere.

"What do you want Sam? I'm busy." He told her.

Sam waved her hand dismissively. "You can stop doing whatever you're doing." She sat on his bed and crossed her legs, the pale gold dress she wore showing off a lot of her thigh. "So what's new? We hadn't *hung out* in a while. I figured you missed me too."

Shawn arched a brow. "I've been focused on other things."

"Other things like that tart you're panting after!?" Samantha hissed. "Maybe I should turn her into a toad? Maybe that'll help you get your priorities straight!"

"No, but it'll definitely get your eye swollen shut." Natori growled as she stalked into the room.

Shawn stood. "Tori! To what do I owe the honor? Finally considered my offer?"

"I'll speak with you about that later." Natori told him, her eyes never leaving Samantha.

Sam smiled condescendingly. "What part did you walk in on? The part where I called you a tart? Or the part where I said I'd turn you into a toad?"

Natori smirked. "Are you that insecure? That you would threaten to turn other girls into animals? If Shawn loved you as much as you think he does, he wouldn't have you embarrassing yourself like this. If *any* guy loved you, they wouldn't do what he's doing. Shawn doesn't care anything about you. To him, you're old news. Why don't you stop wasting your time with him and find someone who actually cares? That being said, you ever threaten me again and I hear it, or someone comes to me with something you said, I will rip you to shreds. I have bigger problems, and you are not, nor will you ever be one of them. Now Shawn, we really need to talk."

"And what would you know about it? You're untouched! A baby in this! Don't speak on things you don't know."

"I clearly know more on this topic than you, otherwise I would probably let some guy treat me like I'm trash for little more than to improve my status as well."

Samantha growled, and conjured a fireball. Throwing it, she watched as it hit Natori and sent her slamming into the nearby wall. She smirked, and then frowned as the smoke cleared. Natori was on her feet, and unharmed. Not even her clothes were singed.

"You... Dumb... Bitch." Natori growled. "My infinity is fire." Natori rushed forward and punched Samantha. The force of it knocked Samantha to the floor, and Natori tackled her. Straddling her waist, she wailed on Samantha.

Shawn winced with every hit that landed. He could see Samantha scratching at Natori, but Natori's fists kept knocking her off balance. He watched as her hands clamped tightly around her neck. He knew he should stop her before she killed Samantha, but this was the time to access both her strength and weakness. When he had gathered enough information, he rushed over and pulled Natori off. She struggled furiously, and broke loose long enough to grab Samantha's hair. Shawn wrapped his arms around Natori's waist and pulled, and Natori used her other hand to punch Samantha in the head repeatedly. He noticed the redden skin where Samantha raked her nails across Natori's arms and face.

"Bitch I'll kill your motherfucking ass!!!" Natori yelled as Shawn finally managed to pull her off.

Jikiya rushed into the room then, and stopped at the sight of his struggling grandniece and a barely breathing Samantha. He looked into Natori's eyes, and his own filled with a profound sadness. He walked over to Samantha and lifted her into his arms. He left the room as quickly as he had come. Samantha needed medical attention immediately.

130

He could see the hand-shaped burns around her neck. When they were gone, Shawn quickly released Natori. He wouldn't comment on how she was a perfect fit in his arms.

"Told her. Now Shawn," Natori called, perfectly calm. "Something's happened to my friend, Y'know, the one from Cassie's party? And your clan is responsible. I need answers, and I need them now."

"And if I refuse? Will you beat me like you did Samantha?" He asked, he had to be sure.

Natori smirked sadistically. "I could… But no, I'll just let my sadist great grandfather headmaster Pyro have you. I am the only thing standing between you and the possibility of you becoming one of his trophies. Have you seen his work? He's *amazing* at mutilation."

"I'll answer any questions you have!" Shawn replied quickly, having his confirmation.

"I thought you would see things my way." Natori smiled. "As for your earlier question… Yes, I have considered your offer, and my answer is yes. I think us being friends would be a wonderful idea."

It was well after dark when Alex and Ashten walked into Pyro's office. They had been gone since the early part of morning patrolling the forest and eliminating the intruding Takahashi. Pyro was leaning against his desk with the sleeves of his white dress shirt rolled up. He was reviewing a student file, and didn't look up at either one of them when they entered. The twins bowed and lowered their heads, as was custom whenever Pyro was in full-blown leader mode.

"Did you two take care of the situation?" He asked, not looking up from the file.

"Yes *Starší*, all of the intruders have been eradicated. We also found out that they were trying to make contact with Natori through her dreams. As well as create a route for her to take had she ran out of the manor with the intentions of quickly saving Connor. They intended to kidnap her and drag her to their realm to kill her." Alex informed.

Pyro nodded. "Training and preparations for liberation will begin tomorrow. I need you two rested and ready to train Natori. I would have liked to have given her more time to get acquainted with her powers, but time is of the essence. If we don't get to Connor within a certain time limit they will kill him… And thank you."

Alex and Ashten nodded and stood, walking out of the office door. They passed Demetrius, who was entering as they were leaving. He hugged both of them, and then turned to his brother.

"Did you find anything?" Demetrius asked.

"Yes." Pyro sighed, passing him the file. "Prepare your knives brother. We have a traitor in our midst."

Chapter 11

"You are not unworthy of the power; the power is unworthy of you."

The rain had soaked through the clothing of everyone enduring the storm. Every guardian of the Sukimori tribe had gathered in the training grounds. Natori stood before her leaders, her face a mask of determination and her body the epitome of tense.

"I did not want to have to do this… But time is not on our side, and we need to prepare our crown as soon as possible. There are some things that some of us excel at, and as such, it will be quicker if each person trained her in the area they are best at. Blake, you are the most skilled in bonding, so you will take over." Pyro sighed, looking up to the weeping sky.

"Elder… This is… Dangerous…" Sebastian whispered quietly, but Pyro heard him.

"We know Sebby, but with the amount of time we *do* have…" He started.

"We can't afford to consider the dangers at this time." Demetrius finished.

"So, what am I learning first?" Natori asked.

"Draw your sword. Your next lesson is bonding. Your soul is already a part of the blade, but that was only part of it. Now, you need to bond with it fully. Blake will take it from here." Pyro told her, stepping aside as Blake stepped forward.

Natori wordlessly drew her sword, marveling once again at the thick blade that shined bright even amid the gray sky. The onyx rose at the bottom of the blade shimmered slightly, and the white and red ribbons that hung from the bottom of the handle coiled around each other. A bad feeling spread through her, but she ignored it. Connor was in pain, and she would jump in front of a speeding car for him. She parted her legs and bent slightly; changing positions to see which one would work best. Natori smiled when she took her final position, she held the sword horizontally and parallel to her face. Both hands held the handle firmly and her legs were shoulder length apart and bent slightly.

"Alright, the way this works is that your blade is like an appendage of yours. You need to form a connection with your limb, like how the brain sends signals to different parts of your body? It's the same concept with your sword. Your soul is already bonded with it; we just need your mind and body to bond with it as well. Got it?" Blake explained.

Natori nodded and relaxed her positon. She then closed her eyes and took a deep breath and focused on the auras that emitted from her sword. She felt the familiar electric aura that was her soul, and then there was another, much darker presence. The two auras were clashing with one another, fighting for overall dominance. This wasn't supposed to happen. Creating the two mantras by saying different words should have made the darker aura weaker than her own, but she could feel her own aura struggling. She could see it now, the electric purple aura that was uniquely hers, and the darker force were locked in a power struggle.

"Hurry Natori!" her soul cried out. "Banish it from Růze Trn!"

The two auras became humanoid then, one electric purple shape, and one black shape. The dark shape kicked her aura back. It hit an invisible barrier and dropped to the floor. *"Run!"* it called out.

Natori turned to run, but the shadow was upon her before she could take a step. It reached out and caught the collar of her shirt. *"Did you really think that you could force your will upon me?"* it asked, cupping her face. It turned her facing it and pulled her against it and threw her to the floor. It straddled her. *"You're still an embryo…"*

Natori struggled against it viciously, and the shadow shifted into a smoke that began filling her throat. She struggled to crawl from its hold and breathe, but the smoke increased both in size and pressure. Natori reached out desperately to the other aura that was uniquely hers, but she could see the corruption overtaking it, just like it was overtaking her.

"You cannot win this…" it whispered sweetly in her ear. *"Just give in… You're only hurting yourself…"*

Even though the corruption was overtaking it, Natori could see her soul trying to crawl to her. It was yelling something, but she could hear nothing above the disembodied voice seducing her to darkness. She knew that if she turned, her family would be forced to execute her. That would destroy them, she knew, but she would rather them kill her, than for someone else to do it. Tears filled her eyes. She was a failure, not good enough to be anything other than what she was. A stupid little girl that was in way over her head.

Pyro and Demetrius struggled to keep Akiko from reaching Natori. Soon after entering the depths of her sword, the red ribbon adorning the bottom of the sword had suddenly constricted around her neck. The veins in her arms were visible, and had begun to fill with a thick, black liquid. These were the first signs of corruption, and once it was completed, they would have no choice but to eliminate her.

"Please! If we don't do something she'll be corrupted!" Akiko pleaded, struggling against combined strength of his elders.

"We cannot approach! The risk of more of us being corrupted is far too great! You know this!" Pyro told him.

Shawn walked outside of the manor and looked into the sky. It had been storming pretty badly, but now it was worse than ever. He felt something dark pulling at him, and he smelt the sweet smell of corruption. Following the scent, he found himself walking towards the training grounds. The guardians were there, no doubt training their precious crown jewel. But something was wrong. Pyro and Demetrius were having trouble keeping Akiko back, and the others were watching on fearfully. Shawn looked to Natori, and his eyes widened. He could see the signs of corruption upon her, and her stance was rigid as she somehow kept it from fully taking over. It was a losing battle however, she still had no idea how to use her abilities, and the darkness that was taking control used it well to its advantage. Shawn closed the distance and grabbed Natori's arms. Pulling her close, he dipped his head so that their faces were mere inches apart.

"You should not wield this power…" He whispered to her.

"But I… Am not worthy… Of its purest form…" Natori whispered through her affliction.

"No… This darkness… Is beneath you… Banish it."

"Beneath me…"

Within the depths of *Rŭze Trn*, Natori's eyes widened. Shawn was right. This darkness *was* beneath her. At the time, she was too self-conscious to realize the mistake she was making. But now she knew, she knew that she was a

136

creature of God. She was something not meant for darkness, no matter how self-conscious she felt, she should have trusted the God she served. Growling, Natori struggled to her feet. Static began to form, and an enraged roar left her lungs. The shadow hissed as it become whole once more. It dislodged itself as if she were made of acid. Natori's struggling soul relaxed, and it fused with her. Pastel purple surrounded her form and spread so powerfully that her hair began to lift. Her eyes sharpened.

"You are beneath me! And I banish you from both my sword and my soul!" Natori commanded as she threw her hand forward. An electric purple beam shot from her palm and hit the shadow dead on. It screamed as it was obliterated.

The black fluid evaporated, and the red ribbon uncoiled itself from her neck. It burned away, and the sword reverted to its purest form. The electric purple outlined both her and her sword, and then gently faded away to nothing.

Shawn watched as Natori's eyes fluttered open, and their gazes locked in amazement. He saw the gratitude and confusion in her eyes, and his own softened endearingly at her untrusting nature. Shawn lowered his head, but he found his arms empty before their lips could meet.

Akiko had broken loose, and had snatched Natori from Shawn. He held his daughter protectively, glaring hatefully at Shawn at his audacity. "Touch her… And what I'll do to you will make Pyro's sadistic fantasies seem pleasant."

Natori shook her head and turned to her father. "No *otec*! Shawn saved my life just now! You would have had no choice but to kill me had he been a second later."

Akiko curled his lip at Shawn. "I understand."

"Good thinking Blake." Pyro told him. "She already knows how to wield her sword; she just needed to bond with it. Now she can use it to its full potential."

Blake nodded. "Yeah. She's a fast learner like Buzzkill. Pretty soon she'll start killing every buzz within a fifty mile radius like her father."

Akiko sighed angrily. "I should have let you drown in the bathtub."

Blake whirled. "You said you wouldn't tell anyone about that! Dude! Does the bro code mean nothing to you!?"

"You told me that you would stop calling me that infernal nickname." Akiko growled.

"I lied!"

"So did I!"

Pyro turned to Jeremiah with an amused smile. "Those are your sons."

Jeremiah sighed. "They have the combined intelligence and attention spans of squirrels."

Blake and Akiko gapped at him.

"Dad!" Blake exclaimed indignantly.

"Dad!" Jeremiah mocked remorselessly.

Natori giggled as she watched her family. It did her good to see that they could goof off, but they had a limited amount of time, and it was not supposed to be used for games. It was only a matter of time before they became bored with Connor. She didn't know what they had planned for him when that happened, and she wasn't willing to find out.

"You guys! Connor's still being tortured! Could we maybe resume my training?"

Pyro's smile slipped a bit at the reminder. "No more today. Take some time and make sure that your bond is intact. You were being corrupted not even two minutes ago. Rest."

Natori nodded and made her way back into the manor with Shawn behind her. Once they were gone, Akiko turned to Pyro. "Do you think it absorbed?"

Pyro nodded. "Yes… It absorbed."

138

Shawn opened the door to the manor, and Natori stepped inside. She was thoroughly soaked and she was sure that she was leaving footprints on the carpet.

"Hey so um... You have some company waiting in your room." Shawn told her.

"Seriously? Ok." Natori sighed. She was soaked through, and wanted to do nothing more but take a shower, change into some dry pajamas, and go to bed. But she had a feeling that this meeting in her room was important.

Shawn led Natori upstairs towards her room, and then grabbed her arm when they reached the top.

"What?" Natori asked him.

"Your sword Tori. You might want to sheath it. You don't wanna scare them now do you?" Shawn replied, gesturing towards the blade that she still had drawn in her hand.

Natori giggled. "As hilarious as that would be... No. At least not at the moment." She sheathed her sword.

Shawn stared at her with a certain hunger in his eyes. It was her only warning before he grabbed her hands and pinned her against the wall. He moved both of her hands to one of his larger ones and pressed her hands above her head.

"What the hell are you doing!?" Natori yelled angrily.

Shawn pressed their lips together, letting his free hand linger on her hip, barely there, but there nonetheless. Natori moaned against her will as the foreign hormones raged through her. She felt as if fire itself flowed in her veins instead of blood. Shawn pulled back slowly, a smile on his face as he stared at the flames in her eyes.

"I wish you could see how beautiful you become... When those carnal emotions awaken... You're even blushing... How adorable." Shawn whispered sinisterly.

"Shawn... You're corrupting me..." Natori sighed, looking away.

"Yeah, but not in the way you're thinking."

"Oh?" Natori inquired. "You don't want sex? You should relay that message to other parts of your body then."

Shawn chuckled, lifting her off of her feet. "Yeah, it is what you're thinking then."

Natori pushed Shawn back. "I'm not Samantha. Touch me again and I'll rip your heart out. 'Kay?" She left Shawn in the hallway and walked into her room. She stopped at the sight of Bryanna and Reeze. "Hey guys! Sorry I haven't spoken to you two in a while… It's just that—"

"Tori, it's alright. We know what happened with your friend." Reeze told her.

"We want to help you." Bryanna added.

Natori smiled softly. "Thanks guys… But we don't even know where he is."

Reeze smiled. "Aren't you glad that you know me?"

"You know where he is?" Natori asked hopefully.

"No, but if you have something that is uniquely his, I can teleport your soul to his location."

Chapter 12

"At any time, your life could change forever…"

Natori's eyes widened, and she smiled hopefully. It was the first real smile she had ever since she had found out about Connor. She was Connor's best friend, and as such she had a lot of things that belonged to him.

"Reeze… You have no idea how much this means to me." Natori told him as she began to rummage through her drawers. Akiko had created an exact replica of her room, but everything except for her furniture was authentic. He had basically transferred her room to the manor.

"Here it is!" Natori exclaimed as she pulled out a folded sheet of paper. She walked back over to Reeze and handed it to him, and he opened it.

'Hey! Hey! Hey! Get well soon! Please? I'm deathly bored without you here! On second thought… Get me sick too, that way we can both avoid the disaster known as Cassie at all costs. Much love! –Connor'

Reeze laughed. "That's cute. Boyfriend?"

"Best friend."

"Sounds like a boyfriend."

Natori rolled her eyes fondly. "Will that work?"

"This is perfect. Handwriting is as 'yours' as it gets. Come here."

Natori walked over to Reeze and sat across from him. He grabbed both of her hands and closed his eyes. Natori closed her eyes as well, hearing the note crumble as it was wedged between their hands. It was dark for a while, and Natori once again felt her soul drifting through the cosmos. It had been a while since her soul traveled through the universe, her soul wasn't falling into the recesses of her mind as it would whenever she regained a memory. It was literally traveling through the universe. This time however, Reeze was traveling with her. She could feel their hands intertwined as they drifted through the realms. It was peaceful. In this moment, she could just relax and forget about everything that plagued her. Her abilities, her destiny, her deteriorating sanity, and the prophecy...

But forgetting wasn't why her soul drifted, and it would do her no good to forget. She had a purpose. A task at hand.

Natori saw a light then, and she shielded her eyes as it became blinding the closer she and Reeze got to it. When the light had finally diminished, she uncovered her eyes and looked around.

It was night where they were, and she appeared to be standing outside a small cottage in the middle of a clearing. As she observed the cottage however, her vision changed. She could still see the cottage, but she could now see the systems of tunnels that lied beneath the surface.

"I can only keep you here for 20 minutes without them detecting your presence." Reeze told her.

"Why?" Natori asked.

"Because your power is greater than mine, I can suppress powerful beings for 20 minutes before their aura begins to overshadow mine. Hurry Tori! Time's ticking!"

Natori nodded in understanding, and ran around the back of the cottage. She could feel Connor's presence within one of the tunnels, and if her guardians were coming to liberate him, then she would need to gather every bit of information she could while she was there. Upon reaching the back of the cottage she saw a generator, and a lush forest surrounded the area. There was also an assortment of weapons and worn out patches in the grass. The guardians could use the forest to their advantage, but she didn't know if her relatives knew anything about these forests. It was fair game. Natori walked through the wall of the cottage. It looked normal enough. Average kitchen, small sofa, a desk littered with papers, a small radio, and a door that led to a bedroom upon inspection. Any normal human would write this off as a regular cottage in the middle of the forest. But Natori wasn't fooled, she felt the amount of violence that had partook here. The feel of death, sorrow, and rage permeated the very air.

Natori checked her watch. 15 minutes left. Damn. She didn't have enough time to personally inspect every tunnel beneath the cottage, and so she closed her eyes, and let her aura spread through the tunnels. She didn't raise it, as not to overshadow Reeze and give her away, but rather let it ghost upon this place, getting a feel of each area and locating Connor faster. A familiar sensation reached her, and she focused on it. Within the longest tunnel, at the very end, was her Connor.

"Did you find him?" Reeze asked.

"Yeah... I found him." Natori replied.

Connor lay on the cold floor of his cell. Silent tears dropped down his face. His body ached in places he hadn't known existed, it was worse than his hard days at football practice. His cuts were also beginning to become infected.

He wouldn't last much longer here, and he was fine with that. He would never betray Natori, and if he had to die to prove that, than he would do so happily. Suddenly, a faint electric purple aura materialized, and Connor trembled at the possibly of his tormentors being ready for another round with him. It was a mist at first, but then it morphed into a shape that Connor knew all too well. Short and curvy, with feminine muscles, the shape regained it colors. Her hair turned into the beautiful white he had missed running his fingers through, and her skin became that gorgeous tanned that lit up his world like nothing before. Her eyes blazed that fiery amethyst that managed to warm his coldest hours, and a light pink color of full lips that he'd only dreamed of kissing. But there was something else, a black rose graced her left cheek, and black, intricate designs raced from her wrists to her arms. Green vines adorned her thighs, and black roses bloomed from the interceptions of said vines. She had changed physically, but somehow, to him, she looked complete.

"Connor?" Natori asked uncertainly, moving closer. She could tell it was him, and her eyes watered at the sight. The same tall, muscular form that had protected her many nights was lying in a heap on the floor. His usually lightly tanned skin was pale, and looking green from infection. His full lips that were always smiling were chapped and caked with dried blood from where multiple punches landed. One of his eyes was swollen shut, but the other one blazed that same sapphire that was always filled with determination and conviction. His black, blue, and purple hair was greasy and covered in dust. Natori sobbed, and sat down with her legs tucked behind her. She then gently moved Connor so that his head rested on her lap.

Connor smiled softly as her scent invaded his nose, it was the same scent of cherry blossoms, and it gave him great comfort to know that she was truly there with him. He felt the tears landing on his cheek, and the shaking of her shoulders. He reached up and cupped her face, reveling in the warm feel of soft skin against his hands that were roughened from football and work. "Hey now, don't cry for me..." He told her, gently wiping the tears from her eyes.

Still they fell. *"This is my fault... They've hurt you... Because of me..."* Natori whispered.

Connor laughed. "This? Oh no... It's just a new look I'm trying. I've been really digging the tormented look lately, thought I would call a few people to help me try it out...It isn't really me though."

"Connor this isn't funny!" Natori yelled. *"Now tell me what is this place?"*

"They call it the realm of perpetual night. Darkness reigns here, and this is the home of creatures that would make Michael Myers a preferable choice." Connor covered his mouth and coughed so hard that his body jerked from the force of it. He uncovered his mouth and sighed at the blood that now stained his palm..

"Blood...? Oh Connor, what have they done to you...?" Natori whispered in horror.

Connor smiled sadly. "You don't want to know sweetheart... I'm so happy that you're here... I didn't think I'd ever see you again."

"You weren't supposed to remember me. You were supposed to graduate, go to college, get married, and have little ankle biters running around breaking every piece of furniture they could find... I would have been content to watch you from afar. I never wanted any of this to happen! Connor I'm sorry! I'm so sorry!" Natori sobbed, covering her face in misery.

Connor shook his head. "You were born for this... Walk in your calling Tori, this world needs people like you..."

"Natori, I can only hold it for 2 more minutes." Reeze told her.

Natori nodded to him and closed her eyes. Rage filled every fiber of her being, and she let out a scream that shattered the lights in the room. The sound radiated through the entire cottage and destroyed everything within its reach. It even reached outside and destroyed every weapon the Takahashi possessed and the generator that gave the cottage power. Her soul was the only light within the cell, and Connor watched as Natori straddled him. He could feel her weight pressed against him, and she leaned down and pressed their lips together. Connor closed his eyes and accepted her, feeling a mist enter his body. His wounds healed, and she pulled back.

"I have to go… But I will return… I'm getting you out of here Connor."

"Time's up! I can't hold it anymore!" Reeze told her.

Natori's vision blackened, and the next thing she knew, she was back in her room. She hadn't moved since she and Reeze had soul traveled. She was still holding Reeze's hand.

"What happened?" Bryanna asked after a moment.

"… He's in the realm of perpetual night. Locked in a cell within a system of tunnels beneath a small cottage." Natori told her.

Reeze was silent for a moment, before his eyes snapped to Natori. "Did you destroy everything!?"

Natori looked away guiltily. "Yes… I don't know how I did it… But I did it…"

"They're going to know that you were there… We need a plan." Reeze sighed.

"I've gathered enough intel." Natori said as she stood. She walked over to her dresser and grabbed a sheet of paper and a pencil. Turning on her desk light, she sat at the desk and began to scribble.

Reeze and Bryanna looked to each other, and then back to their friend. They watched as she scribbled like a madwoman until she had finally put the pencil down with a sigh. Natori then stood and made her way back over to them and sat down. She laid the sketching out in front of them. They saw a sketching of a small cottage surrounded

146

by a forest. At the back was a training ground, and underneath was a system of tunnels. There was a circle drawn at the end of the longest tunnel. Other circles were drawn at different points within the forest.

"Natori... What is this?" Bryanna asked.

"A plan, and a really good one if I do say so myself." Natori replied with a humorless smirk.

"Oh my God... Natori this is brilliant! You're a genius!" Reeze exclaimed.

Natori chuckled. "Father says that I was a tactician in my past life."

"He'd be right, Natori this is almost a guaranteed victory! We gotta show this to the others!"

Natori rolled up the strategy, and the trio rushed out of the room and dashed down the hall. Their footsteps were surely louder than the raging storm as they pounded down the stairs and ran towards the headmaster's office. The other guardians had been within the confines of Pyro's office, drying themselves off from the storm. The door was thrown opened so suddenly that it startled the others as three beloved brats burst into the office panting out gibberish. Natori was waving a rolled up paper about.

"Hey! Hey! Hey! Calm down! Catch your breaths and gather your collective thoughts, and then *calmly* tell us what has transpired." Pyro told them.

After calming themselves, the trio recounted the events leading up to their dramatic entrance. The others listened attentively to every word spoken, letting all that they had been told sink in. Pyro sat at his desk and rubbed his temples. He pointed to the three chairs that were in front of him, and the younger beings sat down. Her relatives leaned against various things, and silence was the only noise. Finally, Pyro sighed. "That was very reckless and I would advise you not to try that again without one of us present... But it did work in our favor. Let me see your game plan."

Natori handed him the paper, but Pyro grabbed her wrist. He was still for several heartbeats as her ordeal replayed in his mind. When he let go, he was glaring at her. "You destroyed their hideout?"

"I-I don't know how I did it… I didn't mean to I swear! It just happened."

"You need to learn to control that temper of yours. I also know what you did to Samantha, but that is a conversation for tomorrow." Pyro scolded, grabbing the blueprint. He nodded with a smile. "Has your father ever told you that you might have been a tactician in your past life?"

"Yes sir." Natori replied with a smile.

"This is absolutely brilliant. We just need to make a few backup plans and discuss this further and we'll be ready to get your friend. Now everyone gather around, and I would also ask that no one else within this manor is shown these strategies."

"But elder… Why? Would it not be helpful to have allies other than ourselves?" Natori asked.

"Someone has betrayed us. And while I would normally welcome other allies, we cannot risk the chance of being exposed. Of course this doesn't include the Eastern Lycan tribe or the northern warlocks. I would welcome their help, with that being said Reeze and Bryanna, I want you two to talk to your parents after we solidify this."

Reeze and Bryanna nodded with narrowed eyes, and Natori's eyes widened.

"Who would do such a thing!? After all your tribe has done for us!" Bryanna growled, her eyes glowing. "Do you know who it might be?"

"I believe so." Pyro sighed. "But I am not sure…"

"And when you are sure? What will we do then?" Natori asked, crossing her arms.

Pyro shrugged. "Hm. Well Jesus would turn the other cheek and let God deal with them… But I'm not Jesus so they're dead bitches when I find them. But that too, is a conversation for another day. Right now, we have to polish this." Pyro said, holding up the blueprints.

The group gathered around Pyro's desk and discussed the strategy in detail, adding factors that Natori hadn't thought of at the time. When it was done, the original tactic was more detailed, and there were two backup plans in place in case the original plan fell through. There were copies made in each person's individual language, and the original plan was incinerated. This was so that in the event that the traitor got ahold of someone's copy, decryption would be impossible.

"Wow… Who knew that made up languages would come in handy." Blake asked aloud.

Back upstairs, the door across from Natori's room opened, and Shawn stepped out. His cellphone was pressed against his ear.

"They've made plans… Get ready, they're coming for him."

Chapter 13

"What's done in the dark always comes to the light..."

Natori felt as if her lungs would burst. She had been underwater for two hours. The day had started with Akiko waking her early to tell her that she would absorb water today. Of course she had asked if it were absolutely necessary since they were to also begin their journey into the realm of perpetual night that day. She was told that it was traditional for Sukimori to have at least absorbed one element before going on their first mission. Since she already had her infinity with fire, they would only need to have her absorb one element. Water had been decided because it was the exact opposite of fire, and would naturally take the longest to absorb. Now here she was, submerged within the deepest lake in the realm. Of course she wasn't alone; Akiko was with her, holding her in his arms. It was to both monitor her progress and keep her from rushing to the surface for air. Pyro was a few feet behind him to make sure that Akiko didn't rush to the surface to get her some air either. It would halt the

151

absorption process and she would have to restart. Once she absorbed the water into her form, she would be able to breathe underwater without the assistance the other students received from one of her uncles. Of course she had asked why she couldn't simply drink a glass of water or take a shower to absorb it. She had been told that it didn't work that way, that in order to absorb something a Sukimori would need to be in some type of peril. The absorption ability would activate and absorb whatever was endangering their lives. A simple shower or drinking water would not be enough to activate such defense mechanism.

"I know this scary." Akiko told her. "But open your mouth; it'll be a lot quicker that way. I won't let you go. I promise."

Natori looked to her father; she saw how sincere he was. But of course he meant it; she was his only daughter after all. Her gaze swept to Pyro, who had swam forward and cupped her cheek. The gesture was enough to have her open her mouth. Akiko held her close, not wanting to witness her eyes roll into the back of her skull. Her body convulsed, and Akiko felt the urge to swim to the surface hit him like a thousand volts. Pyro held him by his shoulders however, so the urge was impossible to truly carry out. Just as her heart began to stop. It happened.

Her eyes rolled forward, and then tinted to an icy blue. Natori felt the water rushing into every crevice of her body, and she inhaled deeply. Pushing Akiko back gently, she simply stood on the water as if it were the very ground. Breathing was no longer a struggle for her.

"Is this what it's like? To absorb an element?" Natori asked.

"Yes, we wanted you to feel what it was like. You now control fire and water. You will be able to bend both elements to your will and as you have seen with your infinity, you will be able to summon the element from your

152

body. It is why it is best to completely submerge yourself." Akiko told her.

"Come." Pyro called. "The time has come to rescue Connor."

The trio ascended from the watery depths and made their way back to the manor. Natori listened to the sounds of nature as they strolled through the forest. The sound of the wind blowing the leaves, and the grass crunching beneath her feet was a thing of beauty. The magnitude and detail of such creation never ceased to amaze her.

"This will be your first mission. I will tell you now that you may see some horrific things… Do not let it affect your determination." Pyro told her.

Natori nodded solemnly. They were going to travel to the realm of perpetual night to liberate Connor today. It would be a three day journey to the actual cottage according to her father, who had gone prior to scout the lands. From where they would enter, it would give them the element of surprise. No one else knew of these plans nor the exact day they were going except for everyone directly involved. Reeze and Bryanna had gone to talk to their own tribes, and see if they could convince them to help. Natori gasped at a sudden revelation.

"We can access 100% of our brains… Can't we?" She asked Pyro.

Pyro smiled. "When did you realize?"

"I honestly don't know… It just came to me…"

"Well, yes. We can access 100% of our brains. It is why Lucifer threw in that generational curse of mental illness. But see, we turned that curse into a blessing. Yes we still tarry with our random and triggered episodes, but we have converted a curse, something meant to break us, into something that empowers us, a blessing. Of course we could have rebuked it before it took effect, but then we wouldn't be able to complete a mission. If we were to encounter someone with the same affliction, we couldn't tell them how to conquer it in the worst way for the enemy. Who else do you know that is crazy enough to convert a curse into a blessing?" Pyro smirked.

"Only Sukimori… And Connor."

"That is why we were called." Akiko told her. "God knew that we would be crazy enough to do things that other people wouldn't even think of." He ruffled her hair.

When they got back to the manor, Reeze and Bryanna were standing at the door, waiting for them. Natori smiled brightly upon seeing them, and ran into their arms with a happy laugh. They had been gone for weeks, and Natori had missed them terribly. Shawn had kept making underhanded passes at her, and the feeling of distrust grew stronger and stronger the more she stayed with him. Reeze and Bryanna were her best friends, and she didn't understand it, but as the weeks turned to months, she had grown to love her quirky friends.

Pyro crossed his arms. "I assume you have returned with a message?"

Reeze nodded. "My father says that he will prepare his armies at once. They traveled to the rendezvous point a day before, and are currently waiting for us to join them. We stand with you."

"So have we." Bryanna said.

Pyro nodded, and headed inside, his descendants following him up the stairs. Bryanna and Reeze broke up at the second floor to their rooms to prepare. Pyro continued climbing the stairs, and Akiko pulled Natori back just as she went to take a step.

"Are you sure about this? You do not have to join this battle." Akiko asked.

Natori smiled. She knew what he was trying to do. He was worried about her, trying to subliminally urge her to withdraw and let him handle their current situation. He knew that she was a skilled fighter, but he was still her father, and did everything in his power to protect her.

154

Natori hugged her father and nuzzled him comfortingly. He engulfed her in his arms and smiled gently. He couldn't help but remember when she was smaller, how she would cling to him for dear life. Now she was grown up. He had to let her go he knew, but it was hard.

"Father... Yes, this is what I was called to do. Please, I know that you love me and only wish to protect me... But let me walk in my purpose." Natori told him.

Akiko kissed her cheek and nodded. She was right after all, she was called for this, and he had to let her walk in her purpose. He shooed her up the steps, and then followed her to the fourth floor of the manor. Sukimori stayed on the fourth floor, while the other students and faculty stayed on the second and third floors.

"Hey!" a voice called out.

Natori turned to see Samantha closing the distance. As beautiful as ever, Sam still gave off a condescending aura. She had healed well from their fight, but she guessed she would after a month of healing. Natori would have none of it. She needed to prepare to rescue Connor, and she would not be stopped by the likes of Samantha and her ignorance.

"I don't have time for you." Natori told her plainly, beginning to walk away.

Samantha rushed forward and grabbed her arm. Natori whirled and shoved her back.

"I'm trying to help you!" Samantha told her.

"Oh this is about to be epic." Natori chuckled humorlessly, crossing her arms.

"I'm not the bitch you think I am."

Natori arched her brow.

Samantha sighed. "Look, I got out of the infirmary a few days ago, and I was going to Shawn's room when I heard him on the phone. Your name came up, and it wasn't good. It sounded like he was giving a report. He told them not to underestimate you, that you have some kind of untapped potential. You shouldn't trust him; he's been watching you and then reporting to someone. Possibly his clan."

Natori crossed her arms and searched through her memory. She remembered her first day of training, where she discovered her infinity. She noticed it, someone watching her. She opened her senses and turned to where the presence was strongest. It was Shawn. He had changed his appearance. His usual ruby tresses had been black, and his eyes had been green. But even so, his aura was unmistakable. She traveled deeper into her memories, and found Shawn in every situation. She had gone back to the day she had sped home in a panic. Again, amongst the other auras she had felt, was Shawn. He had been there, trying to abduct her along with the other dark creatures that had cleverly hid Shawn's aura from her uncle. Rage caused Natori's eyes to tint a deep red, and she glared at Samantha in her anger.

"That... Bastard..."

Samantha stepped back. "You believe me?"

"The proof that I needed was embedded within my memories. So yes, I believe you. But why? Why would you expose your boy toy to someone you hate?"

Samantha crossed her arms. "Because it took someone I hated to make me realize that I hated myself even more."

Natori nodded. "Yeah well, thanks."

"This doesn't make us friends. Just doing you a favor." Samantha growled.

Natori laughed. "Spare me, please. I would never place my trust in someone like you unless I saw the proof of your words myself."

The two went their separate ways, and when Natori had reached the fourth floor she took a detour. She bypassed her room completely, and quickly made her way to the room at the end of the hall and knocked on the door to her left. It opened to reveal Pyro, dressed in a black Sashinuki.

156

He wore no shirt, and his hair was pulled back into a ponytail.

"Tori? Why aren't you prepared?"

"Because I need to inform you about the latest development of our situation."

Pyro nodded. "Come in."

Natori strolled into the room and marveled at the royal walls. She noted the black dressers that were decorated with framed pictures of her family in many different places. Natori grabbed a frame off of the dresser and examined it. It was a picture of them all at the beach, and everyone had their own pose. Her father was laughing at Pyro, who was holding her up on his shoulders with a wide smile. Natori's hands were stretched high, and she grinned like the elated child she was. She remembered this. It had been her seventh birthday, and her father had taken her to the beach as a surprise, hence the sandy ground and the sun setting over an endless ocean in the background. It also explained the reason why they wore swim suits. She had always thought that it had been just the two of them, but as it turned out, her entire family had come to celebrate. Even her mother, who had been hiding all this time, had risked her life to celebrate her daughter's birthday. She was in her father's arms, laughing as her curly orange hair blew in the wind. The world blackened once more, and Natori felt her soul falling back. The curtain once again parted, and she viewed her newly recovered memory.

'Natori screamed happily as she ran on the sandy beach, looking back to see her great grandfather chasing after her. Today was her birthday, and as a surprise, her father and mother had taken her to the beach. Her family had been there upon their arrival, and Natori hugged each and every one of them. A pair of arms caught her from behind, and she screamed as she was lifted and placed on her great grandfather's shoulders. They had played and danced all

day, and now it was almost time for them to go back to the hotel to eat.

"Let's get a picture before we go!" Demetrius called as he set up the camera.

Pyro walked over to the others, bouncing a giggling Natori as he went. Once he was there, they all posed, and both Akiko and Chikara laughed when Natori had made a silly face. Demetrius had set the timer, and then quickly found his place beside his older brother.

The camera flashed...'

And Natori was back. She gazed at the picture with a new found light, and smiled gently in remembrance of what had truly happened that day.

"... They love each other... My mother and father..." Natori said quietly.

Pyro looked over her head at the picture and smiled. "Your father is the sun to your mother. Your mother is the air your father breathes. You are both the sun and the air to them both. That is why they chose to hide you, so that you may live. Now, what did you want to tell me?"

Natori put the frame back in its place and turned to her leader.

"I know who the traitor is."

Pyro's eyes narrowed. "Who?"

"Shawn Marshall."

Chapter 14

"There are some things that one is willing to die for…"

The door to Natori's room opened just as she clamped on the second anklet. She turned to see Shawn closing the door. Pyro had told her to act natural, but her blood boiled at the sight of him. However, she knew to keep her temper in check, or else he would know that something was off.

"Hey. Why are you here?" Natori asked, her voice slightly clipped.

"You're upset." He noted, noticing the tone of her voice.

Natori nodded. "I just want to rescue my friend. I'm sick of demons torturing him just so they can lure me to them."

"I'm sure anyone would be upset about that."

"Mhm."

Shawn closed the distance between them and put his hand on her upper arm. "I'm worried about you." He told her.

"I'll be fine. I've been training for moments like these for a very long time." Natori replied as she made sure that her thigh sheaths were secure.

Shawn wrinkled his brow. "How long?"

"Since I was four." She answered, strapping Růžé Trn on her back.

"Of course, I wouldn't expect anything less from Akiko. But please, be careful. Don't get yourself killed."

Natori rolled her eyes. "The only people getting killed are those bastard Takahashi and *anyone* dumb enough to help them." Natori growled as she left the room. Her eyes were red by the time she exited the manor. Upon reaching the training field, she saw that a portal was open, as well as her battle ready family and friends. "Hey." Natori chirped as she stood beside Reeze and Bryanna. Who both wore leather suits.

"Ooh! You've gone all 'sexy tribal warrior princess' on us! I like!" Reeze exclaimed.

Natori simply rolled her eyes fondly.

"Did everyone memorize our plans?" Pyro asked.

"Yes elder." They collectively replied.

"Good. The portal is ready and our allies are waiting. Let's go."

Natori nodded, stepping up to the portal. She sighed and looked back at the school. There were innocent beings inside, ignorant of everything that has happened. She wanted to keep it that way. Shawn watched from the window as the Sukimori tribe, as well as Reeze and Bryanna departed. The portal closed, and it was as if nothing had happened. Grabbing his cell phone, Shawn dialed a number.

"Hey. They're gone. I don't know how much time you all have, but use it to prepare."

Connor lied in a heap at the corner of his cell. He didn't know how much more he could take. They had come earlier with the intent to most likely kill him, but then they left. This place was eating at his sanity the longer he stayed.

He could feel Natori's soul shining within him, and he could sometimes hear her praying for him. He took comfort in her words of celebration, of thanks that their mission was victorious and that he was liberated. She was coming for him; he could feel it with every fiber of his being. Shawn had been gone for a while now, spying on Natori, he had no doubt about that. Connor could still remember what Shawn had told him the night before he left.

'Your precious little Tori trusts me… So much so that she let me kiss her… I'm going to make her fall in love with me, and she'll forget all about you.'

Connor had laughed in his face. He knew her better than anyone save her own father. She didn't place her trust in just anybody, much less her love. He knew that his Tori didn't trust Shawn, even now; he smiled humorously at the thought. As if Natori could ever love a man like Shawn. His double life wouldn't be a secret forever, and when she did find out, he would be a dead man. A tremor went through his body suddenly, and then a warm feeling spread through him. He knew the feeling well.

Natori was near.

It was faint, so he knew that she wasn't as close as he wanted, but in the same place. Relief washed over him as he leaned against the oak beam. Closing his eyes, he slept his first peaceful sleep, knowing that nightmare that was this cell would soon be over.

"King Pyro! We've scouted the lands and have caught the collective scent of the Takahashi demons." A voice called soon after the Sukimori exited the portal.

"Thank you Travis. I am sure that your packs are on top of things." Pyro replied, his eyes on Natori.

Travis was the leader of the eastern lycan tribe, and a close ally of the Sukimori tribe. His short hair was black, and his eyes were inhumanly green. He was also Bryanna's father, and the two could be easily mistaken as twins.

Natori stood away from the others, gazing up at the dark sky. The stars shined bright enough to make seeing the landscape easier. Reeze and Bryanna flanked her sides. Travis followed Pyro's line of vision to the young girl of prophecy.

"I see the prophecy has been fulfilled... Your great granddaughter is a lot like her father, in a state of constant thoughts." Travis mused.

"I'm guessing you caught her scent? Which is how you know that Akiko's her father right?"

"Yes."

Pyro nodded and turned his gaze to Akiko. He was standing off as well, leaning against the closest tree with his eyes closed. No doubt deep in his own musings. If not for their stark contrast, they would be mistaken for clones.

"I am worried about her. The Takahashi have resorted to dirty tricks. They kidnapped her friend in order to draw her out. She is a smart girl, but reckless. I am afraid that she may sneak off in the night."

"Do not worry about such things my Lord; I am sure that my daughter and Reeze will not allow something like that to happen. Natori is a very intelligent girl. She may be reckless, but I'm sure she'll think twice before acting. Besides, she knows that if she dies it'll jumpstart Armageddon. She wouldn't be so reckless as to throw *all* caution out the window. Trust her."

Pyro nodded. "You are right old friend. Now, where are the northern warlocks?"

"It's their turn to assume watch duty. We were about to fetch dinner if you are hungry."

Pyro chuckled. "Yes, we are hungry."

Metal clashed suddenly, and the leaders turned to see Natori and Jikiya locked dagger to blade. Intrigued, Pyro watched the exchange closely. Of course Jikiya was

162

physically stronger, and had years of experience to his advantage. Natori however was shift. She was also patient and graceful, something she no doubt obtained from her father. Her grace allowed her to dodge Jikiya with ease, while her patience allowed her the wisdom of either tiring her opponent out or waiting for them to make a mistake. Jikiya moved, and Natori caught his wrist. Pyro shook his head; Jikiya never was one for patience. She turned and had her dagger pressed to the vein in his neck. Her eyes widened suddenly, and Pyro knew that she had realized her mistake. Jikiya's arm was around her waist, and his blade was pressed to her stomach. One wrong move and she was dead. She knew that. Natori cursed as she and Jikiya separated.

"You are skilled, but you still have much to learn in the ways of combat." Jikiya told her.

"Yeah… Skills are nothing compared to experience. Maybe Shawn was right; maybe I should have stayed behind." Natori sighed.

Jikiya's lip curled. "Don't let that sniveling swineherd take you out of your focus Tori. We were all inexperienced once."

Natori smiled. "You're right! Sorry! I guess I'm a little nervous… This being my first mission and all."

"And I can't read!" Blake randomly exclaimed.

Pyro turned to his third grandson, mouth agape. "No you didn't…"

Laughter erupted from the group, and Natori shook her head fondly. That was her uncle Blake.

Later that night had followed Natori out of the camp. Dinner had been served and eaten, and the fire had died a while ago. But sleep wouldn't touch her with a ten foot pole. So, she decided to go for a walk. Her walk had taken her to a lake that glowed in the dark naturally. It wasn't too far from the encampment, but far enough. Natori sat down and bought her knees to her chest. So much had happened

163

in so little time, it was amazing that she could even process it all. But she knew that she was still a long ways off from being what she needed to be. She still had so much to learn.

"God? Listen… You know this the first time I've poured my heart out to you like this but… I just need to know if I'm doing the right thing… I mean, they're torturing my best friend! If you're supposed to know me better than I know myself then you must know what he means to me! Please… Just let me know that I'm on the right track…"

Go with my love daughter, and know that I am with you.

Natori smiled to herself, looking up at the figure that sat down beside her.

"Hi Papa. Why aren't you sleeping?"

Akiko smiled. "I could ask you the same thing sweetheart. Why aren't you sleeping?"

Natori shrugged. "I'm not sleepy. Well… I can't sleep."

"Why?"

"I don't know… I feel a little… I don't know. As if an impending moment is coming. Something that will change everything."

Akiko nodded. "Empathy can sometimes be frustrating. However, this should not make you fearful. God will see us through, no matter what may happen. Now come on, we need you to be fully alert when we face the Takahashi."

Akiko stood, smiling as he helped Natori to her feet. She sighed, and followed her father back to the camp site. She had gotten her confirmation. Now, she was going to make the Takahashi wish that they were never born.

Chapter 15

"The only certain thing is uncertainty."

Three days had come and gone like quicksilver. Natori and the others had been training for this moment. She, along with Reeze and Bryanna led the way seeing as they were actually there at one point.

"It's just beyond these trees." Reeze said as they stepped beyond said trees.

The cottage was there, standing plainly in the dead of night. Natori moved forward, but a hand stopped her from taking another step.

"Wait. It's a glamour. Dissolve it." Akiko told her.

A glamour, much like the one the snake woman tried to trick her with in her dream. Natori's eyes narrowed and she saw the ripple slightly distorting the door. It was the one thing out of place among the otherwise perfect illusion. Natori watched as the cottage shattered like glass. It revealed a houseless clearing, and the army of Takahashi demons that were awaiting their arrival. They all had black hair and white eyes, so it was pretty easy to tell the demons from their allies.

"What? Are you all the welcoming committee?" Pyro asked.

"Sure. Welcome to your death." The demon shrugged.

Pyro laughed. "That's cute."

Natori stepped forward, drawing their attention to her. Her eyes were slowly tinting red. She was tired of this slow ride to hell.

"Give. Him. Back." She growled, unsheathing her daggers.

The demon smirked. "So this is the princess of legend? Hm. Funny. I didn't think you'd be this gorgeous. Too bad we have to kill you… You look like you'd taste like the pink starburst."

"Does it look like I wanna flirt with you? Give him back!"

"Zulo. Stop stalling." A new voice entered the conversation.

Natori knew that voice all too well. They all knew who had spoken. Zulo smirked as Shawn walked over to him. It was a wonder as to how Shawn ended up with red hair and gold eyes if he was a part of the Takahashi clan like the others. Two other demons followed Shawn's lead, and they were dragging someone by their arms. Black hair dyed purple at the ends and the bang dyed blue, deep sapphire eyes, and tawny skin due his long days of practice…

"Connor!" Natori exclaimed.

Connor looked up at the voice. He smiled at Natori gratefully. "Wow… You look… Great…" He panted.

Natori shook her head. He looked so frail, like he'd break at any moment. He was exhausted, she knew that. Her tears welled, and then spilled from her eyes. She hated to see him so broken and beat up. He didn't deserve such a fate.

"Connor… It's alright now… You're leaving this place today!"

Shawn smirked. "Such truth to those words… We only needed Connor long enough to draw you out. Now that you're here… We don't need him anymore." Shawn revealed the dagger he carried and stabbed Connor in the chest. "Goodbye Connor."

166

Natori's chest clenched as Connor's eyes widened. The two demons holding him upright let him go, and Connor collapsed onto the ground, unmoving. The silence was loud, and something within Natori shattered. Her eyes blazed black with a hatred she had never felt before. The electric purple of her aura outlined her body and spread out. Her enraged roar was borderline demonic as she charged. The others followed suit, and in moments the ground was bathed in blood. Natori fought with white hot fury, her clothes splattered with the blood of her enemies as she slaughtered them. Many of them had begged her for mercy, but she had none to give. She dodged a sword meant to decapitate her, and slashed her daggers across the demon's stomach. Her aura that covered the daggers burned the demon from the wound through his entire body. She righted her position and charged towards the Takahashi sneaking behind her fighting brother Sebastian.

Sebastian had dispatched the demon he was fighting, and then turned to see Natori leap onto the demon about to strike him down. Her aura had begun to burn him, and his screaming was cut by Natori's blade slashing across his throat. Sebastian's eyes widened as he noticed the black, soulless eyes. Her psyche had been broken, and she had lost control of herself. He wondered if anyone else were in this state of psychotic rage. But he was in the heat of battle, and could not focus nor bring her back from the dark place she had tapped into.

Zulo's eyes widened as he watched Natori purifying his men. He didn't know that breaking her psyche would unlock the powers she had inherited from Chikara. He whirled on Shawn.

"You said that if we broke her she'd be defenseless! How could you miscalculate this!?" Zulo shouted, kicking back a wolf.

Shawn shrugged. "I thought she would! How was I supposed to be sure!? She didn't even know this would happen!"

"Are you scared Zulo? You should be." A new voice seethed.

Zulo turned to see Akiko, but something was wrong. His eyes were as black and soulless as Natori's. Sapphire flames burned on his skin, but he himself remained unharmed. Natori stepped from behind him, and their identical smiles were downright sinister.

"That boy… Was like a son to me… And you abducted, tortured, and then killed him." Akiko said tonelessly.

"What you did to him… Will be a mercy… Compared to what we're going to do to you…" Natori growled, her daggers slick with blood.

Shawn gulped and began moving back slowly. He hoped that they wouldn't notice him making himself scarce. Strong arms caught him by his neck and waist and lifted him off of the ground.

"Hey Shawn where you going!? The fun's just begun!" Pyro exclaimed in crazed glee. He had been wanting an excuse to kill Shawn for a while now, and now he had it.

Zulo looked behind Akiko and Natori to see the others dispatching the last of his men. Bryanna was in her wolf form, and had caught a demon between her powerful jaws. Reeze had used his mind control to take over the mind of the Takahashi he was fighting. Zulo watched his soldier screaming profanities as his own knife pressed against his jugular.

Reeze laughed. "You can bitch and moan all you want. But either way, you're dead."

The Takahashi sliced his throat, leaving a nasty wound that showed the inside of his neck. He gurgled as he fell to his knees, and Reeze watched as he face planted the ground, the life gone from his eyes. Blood splattered Reeze's face, but he paid it no mind as he went on the next target.

168

Zulo looked back to Akiko and Natori. Their faces were splattered with blood, as was their clothing. The grass was stained with blood and covered with demon remains. Some were whole, others... Not so much. Most were nothing but a pile of ash waiting to be blown away by the wind.

Natori smirked. "Was he scared? I bet he was. Was it fun torturing my best friend? I bet you all had a grand time spilling his blood... It's going to be so much fun spilling yours..."

Zulo stepped back. "You call yourselves creatures of the Lord!? He would be appalled!"

Pyro laughed. "Don't you dare talk to us about God! He knows how we are! And we got his stamp of approval long before this moment! But nice try."

"Natori..." A voice called.

Natori's eyes returned to their normal color, and all thoughts of blood and slaughter diminished at the sound of that one voice. She whirled, and ran to where Connor laid in a heap. Sheathing her daggers, she dropped beside him. He was barely breathing, but he was conscious. She knew she couldn't move him, so she instead grabbed his hands.

"Connor! Connor don't worry you'll make it! Just hang on!"

Connor opened his mouth. "No... Too late... I need... To... Tell you something..."

"Anything!"

Connor smiled weakly. "Tori... *Miluji te*... It's always... Been you..."

"Connor..." Natori whispered, speechless.

At that moment, she realized a deep, heart-wrenching truth.

Natori was in love with Connor. She loved him with every fiber of her being. It was why she never found herself interested in anyone else. It was why she got angry whenever he dated other girls. It was why she had tracked him relentlessly, why she became irrationally reckless where he was concerned. It was why their kiss had scorched her very soul. She trembled at the truth, a truth she had realized much, much too late. And the fact that he had said such a thing in her native tongue made it all the more real.

"*Take Miluji te*… I love you too Connor… With all that I am… I love you too…" Natori told him.

Connor stared into her eyes, and his smile could have blinded her if she weren't so used to it.

"Please don't go…" She pleaded with him.

"I have to… But… Kiss me before I do…?"

Natori nodded with teary eyes. She leaned down and pressed their lips together. It burned her so beautifully. It burned her until there was a permanent scar on her heart, and she knew that she would not forget him. Not now, not ever. When she pulled back, he was gone. His eyes were closed, and his chest no longer moved. He was smiling, peaceful, happy. Natori held him to her tightly, and she felt it again. The urge she had felt when she found him in the dungeon. Her scream shook the very ground, and all who heard it felt the raw grief she now experienced. Arms came around her, and she laid Connor to the ground gently before she held onto her father tightly. She sobbed into his chest, and her chest tightened with every sob that shook her. Akiko stood and held Natori tightly, his own teary eyes blurring his vision before spilling down his cheeks.

"He's with God now…" Akiko whispered.

"He didn't have to die!" Natori wailed, her eyes landing on Shawn.

Rage took over again, and she was suddenly straddling Shawn. She unsheathed one of her daggers and raised it above her head. "You bastard! This is all your fault! I'll kill you!"

"Natori wait! I can explain!" Shawn pleaded desperately.

"No! I don't want to hear it! You betrayed us! You should be dead! Not Connor!"

170

"I did it for you!" Shawn yelled.

Natori lowered her dagger in confusion. Shawn took his chance.

"You were struggling to unlock the power you got from Chikara. You needed to lose yourself, to have the power you need in order to defeat the evil coming for you! But you couldn't unlock it! I wanted to help you but I couldn't tell you! It would've blown my cover and they would have killed Connor before it was time! Connor had to die so that he could unlock his true self!"

"… What do you mean by that?" Natori asked him.

"Natori…" Akiko called, and she could by the sound of his voice that his face was ashen. "Connor's body is gone…"

Chapter 16
"Not everything is as it seems…"

Natori looked over to where she had left Connor's body, and he was gone indeed.

"What…? But…" Natori stuttered.

A light shined suddenly, and it caused the night to become day. Pyro kneeled immediately, and his subordinates followed his lead. Two men appeared side by side. The taller, broader man had black hair, and his hard sapphire eyes softened upon looking at them. His tawny skin stretched over hard muscle, and he bore the same markings they did, but his were red.

"Pyro, you have done well. God says that he is pleased and to keep up the good work. Though, you should really work on that sadist side of yours. It's unsettling."

Pyro laughed. "Thank you Michael, but you know my more sadistic nature is just that, sadistic."

"Of course. Shawn, though what you did was extremely reckless, God says that he is pleased with you as well. Though in the future, think before you act. You could have been killed or worse."

Shawn sighed in relief, but nodded his understanding.

Natori had kneeled before Michael as well, but her heart was shattered. First the love of her life was killed, and now she couldn't even bury him because his body had suddenly disappeared. Michael walked over to her and kneeled in front of her, he knew that he would have a particularly soft spot for the only girl in Pyro's clan. He noted the sad tears that streamed down her face. She was utterly destroyed. He cupped her cheek in his hand.

"I had thought that you would be more excited to meet me young one." He told her.

Natori looked at him, but the excitement wouldn't come. Michael the archangel was kneeling in front of her, and yet she could feel nothing but defeat. She shook her head and closed her eyes, not wanting him to see the tears that flowed freely down her cheeks.

"I failed... It's my fault... If we were never friends... None of this would have happened to him..."

"You have not failed Natori. You have found your *parabati*."

Natori looked up and wrinkled her brow. With everything that had happened, she had forgotten all about her unidentified *parabati*.

"If Shawn is my *parabati*... Then I would rather walk this path alone..."

"I didn't say anything about Shawn. You really love him don't you? Connor."

Natori's chest clenched at hearing Connor's name. It was a name she never wanted to hear again. It would cause the burn on her heart to flare. She nodded wordlessly to his question.

Michael smiled, wiping the tears from her eyes before cupping her face in both hands.

"Natori do you want to know a secret? Connor is my son... My biological son."

Natori's eyes widened, but then she scrutinized him more closely. Michael was practically an slightly older version of Connor! Natori turned away at the stark resemblance.

"Natori, everything that happened, was meant to happen."

"… Why did Connor have to die? I was so close to saving him and now he's gone… I can't even give him a proper burial!"

"Because Tori, much like you, he too had to awaken." Michael answered.

He stood to his feet and pulled Natori up with him. They walked over to the second man, who was a younger version of Michael except for the blue bangs and purple ends of his hair and his markings were gold.

Wait… Blue bangs? Purple ends?

Natori's eyes widened, and she hopped into his arms. "Connor!"

"Tori…"

Connor held her tightly, not caring about the blood splattered on her at all. She fit perfectly in his arms. He inhaled her scent, and then kissed her cheek and fisted his hand in her hair. He didn't think that he would ever see her again, and her kiss had scorched his very soul. It burned his heart like a scar, so that he could never forget her.

Natori held him as if her life depended on it. "I didn't think I'd ever see you again!"

"I know… Strange turn of events huh?" Connor laughed.

"Yeah… Jackass."

Natori let go just to look at him. He was completely clean and rejuvenated, and his tattered clothes were replaced with a simple white Sashinuki. His hair was still down his shoulders, and black with blue dyed at the ends of his bangs with the ends at the back were dyed purple. His eyes were still that deep sapphire, and his smile was goofy. She wrapped her arms around his neck. Connor wrapped his arms around her, knowing she had no intentions of letting go for a while. Michael smiled at the sight, she might have been a trained warrior, but she was still fragile and delicate.

"Natori. Connor is your *parabati*. Together, you two will rid this world of evil."

Natori let go and turned to Michael. She nodded to him in understanding, but kept her hands on Connor's wrists so that he wouldn't let her go.

"However," Michael continued. "Natori after this day your psyche will never be the same. You have become stronger due to unlocking your power, but it has already eaten away a large portion of your sanity. You will start experiencing episodes. If you want, Gods says that He can heal you of this infirmary before it makes itself known."

Natori thought about it. All of her family battled with their illness. She had witnessed some of their minor episodes, and has only heard about their major ones. She shuddered at the tales that were told to her. She didn't know what illness she had, and she honestly didn't want to find out. She had a horrible temper already, and she didn't want her illness making that any worse. However, her family took their individual curses and turned it to a blessing. She was sure that they all had been presented with this choice. She needed to become stronger.

"Thank you Michael, but no thank you. Everyone in my family battles this curse, and I will be no different. If they had enough strength to turn a curse into a blessing, then so will I."

Michael smiled. "I admire your conviction. Connor, you have what it takes to help her."

"I will father. We won't let you down."

"I know. You will need much more training Natori, both you and Connor. Shawn was right when he told you that evil was coming. You all need to be ready."

Both Natori and Connor nodded, and Michael disappeared. The light of day remained, forever engraved in the realm. Natori turned back to Connor and pulled him

176

down to her lips. The fire between them seemingly burned brighter than the sun itself. When they pulled back, he tightened his hold on her and rested his head on the top of her head.

"So... Does this mean you're mine?" Connor asked.

Natori pretended to think about it. "Only if you are mine."

Connor laughed. "Baby, I was always yours."

"Ahem." Pyro coughed expectantly.

Natori giggled. "Right. Connor, I want you to meet the rest of my family. And before you get mad saying that I never mentioned them before, I will explain it to you later."

"Alright, sure. But first..." Connor walked over to Akiko and hugged him tightly. "I missed you Kiko. You can't be the father I needed before I understood everything and then just disappear!"

"And you can't grow on me for eighteen years and then all of a sudden die! You jackass!" Akiko exclaimed, tightening his grip.

Connor gasped. "Akiko you're too strong for this! Let go before you crush my windpipe!"

"Oops. I'm sorry." Akiko replied, letting go.

Pyro sighed. "Alright, I'm ready to go back. Let's go." A golden orb formed in Pyro's hand, and when he tossed it a portal formed. He turned to his subordinates with a smile. "Thank you all for helping us achieve victory this day. It could've gone downhill had you all not been present. But this, and all other glory goes to the Lord, fore he delivered our enemies to our hands. I hope you all have a safe journey back, and do not hesitate to call on us for anything."

Everyone stepped through the portal, and was taken back to their individual homes. Upon reaching the manor, Pyro and the others headed inside toward their individual rooms. Of course Connor had asked about his permanent sleeping quarters.

"You'll stay with Tori. Right now, I'm too tired to think."
Pyro sighed.

Natori smiled. "Reeze, Bryanna, I want you two to come
sleep in my room for the day. I don't want anything else to
happen to the ones I love."

"Sure. Who showers first?" Reeze asked.

Natori looked down at herself at the reminder. Blood and
dirt caked her body, and she shuddered at her current
appearance. "This is disgusting! What was I doing to even
get this dirty!? I've gotten into fights before and I've *never*
had this many patches!"

"Tori… We were just at war with the demons that
kidnapped Connor not even an hour ago. Do you not
remember?" Ashten asked.

"No I remember all the way up until they stabbed Connor,
and then there's a blank slot, and then I heard Connor
calling my name. Why?"

The others gave each other grave looks, but Ashten
smiled at her. "Oh no reason darling! You all must be
exhausted, go on to your room."

Connor shrugged. "Well in terms of showers, I
apparently showered in heaven, so I'm good."

"My room. I get the first shower." Natori said.

"This is your house! You'd get the first shower in any
room!" Bryanna exclaimed.

"Eh, true." Natori laughed as she led the way to her room.

Pyro and the others watched them leave, and then turned
to each other. "She doesn't remember fighting. She must
have lost control…"

"But you did too Roro, and you still remember fighting."
Demetrius reminded him.

"This is a sign of her illness…" Akiko mused. "I'll start
researching such things, and see if I can't determine a few
possibilities."

"She didn't show you any signs of her curse when she was
a child?" Pyro asked.

178

"No, she showed multiple signs of multiple illnesses." Akiko answered.

"Father what does that mean? Are you saying that Tori has multiple illnesses!?" Yukaro asked.

Akiko sighed. "No. But it is a possibility. It's the same phenomenon we experienced when we realized that Sebastian didn't suffer from any mental illnesses."

"But with Natori, it could be multiple." Pyro said.

Akiko nodded. "But it's highly unlikely."

Meanwhile, Natori had taken the first shower. The water was borderline scalding. She was overjoyed that Connor was her *parabati*. Hell, she was overjoyed that Connor was alive! Her heart ached when he had died, and then again when his body had disappeared.

"Thanks God, I didn't get the big picture then. But I'm glad things turned out the way that they did. I don't who's all coming for us… But as long as you're with us, I know that we shall prevail."

She washed the blood, dirt, and grime off, and then stepped out of the shower. She exited the bathroom wearing black sweatpants and a white tank top. Connor was lounging on her bed as per usual of him, and she got on the side that faced the wall. Bryanna left her spot at Natori's desk to take the next shower.

"So Connor do you have any friends? Preferably one that looks as good as you?" Reeze asked.

"Sorry Reeze, my friends have no memory of me anymore." Connor told him.

"Wow. So no one can remember you in earth realm?"

Both Connor and Natori shook their heads.

"Connor remembered me, and that's why he was abducted in the first place. How did you know that no one in earth realm would remember you?" Natori asked.

"Because my dad told me when we spoke. Along with why he couldn't be there to raise me, and so he sent Akiko in his place."

179

"What was it like?" Reeze asked.

Connor shrugged. "It wasn't fun. I wouldn't wish that on anybody. Not even Cassie."

Natori and Reeze laughed, and Bryanna exited the bathroom in a T-shirt and shorts.

"Woo! Bryanna's thick!" Natori exclaimed, trying to move from her place beside Connor.

Connor held her back. "Natori is very *hands-on* if you catch my drift! Run while you can!" Connor called, wrapping his limbs around her struggling form.

Bryanna laughed. "Tori molest me tomorrow! I'm tired."

Natori relaxed, and Connor let go. She turned facing the wall. "I know what you mean. Pick a spot, my bed's big enough."

Reeze took his shower and then joined the others. He used his telekinesis to turn out the light and they were asleep in seconds. Natori had turned and lain on Connor's chest, protecting him even in her subconscious. Connor awoke in a cold sweat. The hell he had been put through was embedded in his mind, and it replayed itself in his subconscious. He looked over to see large amethyst eyes staring back at him.

"Sorry. I didn't mean to wake you." Connor told her.

"It's fine." Natori told him. She moved her head from his chest to the crook of his neck, letting her breath ghost over his neck every time she breathed. It was something her father had done whenever she had a nightmare. It ensured her that he was there and that he wouldn't let anything happen to her. Connor closed his eyes and sighed, and soon enough he slept once more. Natori nuzzled him gently before closing her own eyes, drifting back into the depths of her subconscious.

Chapter 17

"Sometimes in order to find yourself you must leave your comfort zone…"

"Good job Tori, you're absorbing the earth element well." Blake told her.

They were outside in the training field. Blake's hand was encased in stone, and he rested it on Natori's shoulder. Natori stood beside him, absorbing the earth element through him. The elder members of the Sukimori clan thought that Natori had been through enough for the moment, and had ultimately decided to let her absorb the element from them. Being Sukimori, she would be able to absorb the element through the other members. However, she would absorb the last two elements she needed from the members who had that infinity. Otherwise, she would take the ability as well as the element away from the person she had absorbed it from. Absorbing the element from her kin with that infinity however, would prevent such things.

Connor and Akiko stood a little ways off, watching the process intently.

"So," Akiko begin. "When did you realize that you were in love with Tori?"

Connor shrugged. "7th grade. We were walking down the hall, and the light had hit her face… I thought that she was the most gorgeous creature in the universe. I thought that my heart would explode from how hard it was beating. I realized that she was all that I had ever wanted. But I was dating Cassie, and I loved her too."

"Is that why you guys stopped being friends for a while?"

"Yeah, it was mostly my fault. Cassie was downright terrorizing her and I was too whipped to see it."

Akiko placed his hand on Connor's shoulder. "It's in the past now. She's yours, and I know that you will take care of her."

Connor's gaze never left Natori. "Always."

"Hey buzzkill! You're up!" Blake called out.

Akiko growled. "I hate that damn name."

Connor laughed as Akiko strolled over. He turned when someone touched his shoulder. Shawn stood behind him, and Connor's face hardened with contempt.

"What do you want?" Connor asked, not bothering to hide his irate.

Shawn's eyes narrowed. "I did you a favor. You should be grateful!"

"Yes, because torturing me for days on end is such a good thing to do to someone you claim to be helping."

"I was the only one who knew what you were. If the others had found out, they would have killed you long before Natori could save you! I was the sole reason for your survival!"

Connor's face reddened with pint up fury. "It was you that stabbed me in the chest! It was you who tortured me the most! Or did you forget about that? My sole reason for living is over there absorbing the wind element! Not you! Why? If you were so busy helping me, why torment me as harshly as you did, and don't say it was to prove yourself to them, because you did that when you told them about us in the first damned place!"

182

Shawn sighed. "Because... You have something I want."

"And that is?"

"Natori."

Connor laughed. "I knew you couldn't make her fall for you. She would never love a treacherous little bitch like you."

"This treacherous little bitch kissed her, and from my point of view, she enjoyed it. Plus I saved her life! She was beginning to trust me! But one look from you... And she was lost to me forever."

Connor punched Shawn in the face. "Fuck you Shawn." He spat hatefully. "I've loved her for a very long time, and now she's mine. I won't let you take her from me. Touch her again, and I will kill you. Oh, and FYI, she may have liked kissing you, but she *loves* kissing me."

Shawn wiped his bloody mouth and smirked. "So protective... Am I a threat?"

"The only thing you're a threat to is your intelligence," Natori said as she made her way over to them. The usual venom in her voice was gone. "Shawn listen. Not only did you save my life, but you helped me find my *parabati*. For that, we will always be friends. But, I could never be with you. You helped the Takahashi abduct, torture, and kill my Connor. I understand why you did it now, but still... Besides, my heart is spoken for. I'm in love with Connor. And for that, I am truly sorry. That being said, you two need to start getting along. We're in this together. So get it together. We can't face whatever we need to face if we're forever at each other's throats. So stop it. I mean it. Get it together." Natori told them both sternly.

Connor sighed. "When you're right, you're right. Shawn, I am grateful, but you tortured and killed me. I can't just let that slide so easily."

Shawn nodded, and then turned to Natori. She really was beautiful, no matter how average she thought she was. "It wasn't easy doing that to you Connor, but I actually came

183

out here to tell you that Pyro and Demetrius wants to speak with you. Akiko! They said it's time! Whatever the hell that means…"

"Don't worry about it Shawn I know what it means." Akiko told him, signaling for Natori and Connor to follow.

Akiko led them into the manor, and Natori was deep in thought the whole way. She wondered what 'it's time' meant. She hated not knowing things, it made her feel ignorant.

"What's wrong? You're getting frustrated." Connor asked.

"I'm trying to figure out the meaning of 'it's time'. Time for what? We've rested for a week, and then training resumed. I've absorbed all four elements, and you've been learning extensive hand-to-hand combat. Do they feel that we're ready for another mission? And if not, then what? Are they going to tell me about my curse? I know father has been researching on my sudden lapse in memory. Do they sense that I'm about to have my first episode and seek to isolate me from the others? No. Because if that were the case, then you would not be joining me there. All in all, I'm confused and I hate it." Natori growled.

Connor smiled endearingly. That was his Tori, always overanalyzing something. He wrapped an arm around her waist and pulled her close. He kissed her cheek and gave her the dorkiest grin she had ever saw.

Natori smiled contently and leaned against him. "I'm overthinking again aren't I?" she asked.

"Yep!" Connor chirped.

Akiko chuckled as he opened the door to the twins' office. Upon entering, they saw Pyro leaning on the side of his desk reading a book. Demetrius sat at the desk, going through the lesson plans of each teacher. They looked up when the door opened and smiled.

"Hey guys, thanks for coming." Pyro greeted.

"Of course, Shawn said that you wanted to speak with us." Akiko said.

184

"Did he relay my other message?"

"Yes sir. So, would you like to start? Or should I?"

"You do it. Chikara is your wife."

Natori's eyes widened at the mention of Chikara, and Connor wrinkled his brow.

"Chikara? The priestess? Who is she to you?" Connor asked Natori.

"She's... My mother."

Connor gaped. "Tori... That's three strikes against us. They're going to be coming for us full force."

"Especially now since I've unlocked the powers I inherited from mom, and you're the son of Michael the archangel." Natori agreed.

"That's actually why I need to speak with you. Natori, we haven't taught you everything that you need to know, but your powers are now fully unlocked." Akiko told her.

Natori nodded in understanding. She knew that she was nowhere near where she needed to be. Greater evils than Zulo knew of her and Connor's existence, and staying alive would be harder than ever.

"That being said," Akiko continued. "We figured that it was time to tell you the truth about your mother." He took a deep breath. "As you know, Chikara never truly wanted to leave you. But she had to in order to ensure your survival. She's in a different realm. Now, this particular realm is unknown to everyone but us."

"Us... As in the family?" Natori asked.

"Yes, now, there is a certain key that is needed in order to access this realm."

"Where is it?"

Akiko sighed. "Natori... You have that key."

Natori wrinkled her brow. She would have remembered her father giving her something that important. However, she held no memory of him ever giving her such a thing. But then again, not all of her memories had come back, so maybe that was why she didn't remember.

"There's a locket around your neck." Akiko told her.

Both Natori and Connor looked down, and indeed, there sat a locket that she had no knowledge of ever being there. It was gold, and in the shape of a diamond. Emerald gems outlined it, and an amethyst stone was engraved in the middle.

"I... How come I never noticed this before?"

"Because you weren't ready." Akiko answered.

"Natori," Pyro chimed in. "Keeping Chikara hidden is a big deal. We couldn't afford to tell you for fear of the Takahashi kidnapping you. Now, you and Connor are in danger, and you both are too inexperienced to face it right now. So, using this key, you three will travel to her realm and undergo training. Connor, Chikara's father resides with her, and will teach you everything you will need to know. Natori, you need to be trained in your new abilities immediately. Otherwise, that power will overwhelm and kill you."

Natori gasped. This was all so sudden. She didn't want to leave the friends she had made, but she knew what would happen should she perish.

"... I have to go." Natori conceded.

"I know that you do not wish to go Tori, but don't worry. I will be there as well." Akiko told her. "That's why Pyro said 'you three'. Now let me see the locket."

Natori removed her locket and Akiko took it. He opened the locket, and a light swirled above it. The light was a portal, one that would take her to Chikara. Her mother. Natori hugged her great grandfather and uncle, and stepped forward. But something halted her steps. She had conceded to go, but still she couldn't bring herself to step within the portal. Natori crossed her arms and stepped back. Pyro wrinkled his brow. "You still have doubts?"

Natori groaned in agony. "I want to go! I want to meet my mother! I want to know her personally! I want to see her face and encounter her personality! I want to have my mother in my life! But... I can't. Something's holding me back, telling me that I'm not ready for the things that come with meeting Chikara. I have a lot to learn about the Sukimori clan, and I can't even begin to learn about my other side if I barely know this one. So yes, I want to go. But I won't, not yet. Not when I've scratched only the surface of learning about this clan. I hope you all understand, and I hope she understands... It's not that I'm not ready to meet her, I'm just not ready to face the doors that meeting her would unlock. This decision sits right with my spirit, and it sits right with Holy Spirit."

The room was silent for a moment. Everyone was pondering her decision, and the process made Natori fidget uncomfortably. She would've thought that years of people bullying her made her stronger pertaining to the thoughts of others, but here she was, fidgeting because of the possible things her family could be thinking. She had learned long ago, that silence was ironically the loudest noise. It left room for nothing but her own thoughts, and gave her past the perfect opportunity to remind her of every mistake she had ever made. Every lie she had ever told. Every person she had ever wronged, whether it was intentional or not. It also reminded her of all of the lives she had taken.

'Always remember Láska, a life is a life no matter the form it takes. Taking a life is never an easy burden.' Akiko had told her once.

'But Papa, what about the people who find it easy to take a life?' She had asked him.

'Those people... Are monsters. True monsters, doing what goes beyond their nature effortlessly. Things are not always as they seem. Those who make it look easy may can never forget their face, while others who make it seem hard may actually feel nothing. Pay attention love, because sooner or later, the monster within a person always reveals itself.'

Pyro cleared his throat. "I understand jewel. We will not force you to do something you are not ready to do. Get some rest; we have a long journey ahead of us."

Natori bowed in respect and walked out of the room with Connor at her side. The portal closed, and Akiko gave their leader a worried look.

"Elder…"

Pyro shook his head. "She has made her decision. Besides, she is right. She does have a lot to learn about our clan. There will be others, and she needs to know a lot more than she does now if she is to fulfill her calling."

Akiko sighed and looked to the door his daughter walked out of. The course was set, and no matter what they did, eventually, they would reach the same result. The problem was, he didn't know what that result was. Would she overcome the assignments of the enemy? Or would she eventually fall into their clutches? He hated to dwell on these thoughts, but this was a critical moment. There was a chance that no matter what they did, they would lose her forever.

"I'll be damned; I will protect her, no matter the cost."

Made in the USA
Middletown, DE
07 November 2020

23452720R00106